❧ THE NOVELS, STORIES, SKETCHES AND POEMS OF THOMAS NELSON PAGE ❧.

ON NEWFOUND RIVER

CHARLES SCRIBNER'S SONS

NEW YORK, ❧ ❧ ❧ ❧ 1906

TO THE DEAR MEMORY

OF

ANNE BRUCE PAGE

PREFACE

THE reader will, perhaps, bear in mind that "On Newfound River" does not pretend to be a Novel; but is on its face a "Story,"—a Love-Story if you will—of simple Country Life in Old Virginia. The "setting" is wholly that of the Country, the surroundings are all those of a life far from cities, the incidents are, for the most part, those little commonplace events which might have taken place in a rural neighborhood before the war, where the gentry ruled in a sort of manorial manner and their poorer neighbors bore a relation to them part retainer, part friend.

In preparing a new edition for the press, the author has enlarged the work by certain additions to the Story, with a view to making it

PREFACE

more complete and giving a somewhat fuller reflection of the life it undertakes to mirror, somewhat as he did before with "The Old Gentleman of the Black Stock." But no attempt has been made to change it into a Novel, or even to enlarge it beyond its original scope. It was written as a Love-Story and a Love-Story, pure and simple, it is.

T. N. P.

OAKLAND, Hanover County,
Virginia, 1906.

ILLUSTRATIONS

From Drawings by John Edwin Jackson

ON NEWFOUND RIVER

ON NEWFOUND RIVER

I

NEWFOUND RIVER, or, as it is called by
the denizens of that section of Virginia
through which it glides, "Newfound," steals
through two or three counties of Eastern Virginia in such a leisurely, unobtrusive fashion
that it was not supposed by the early settlers to
be different from the numerous "branches"
which are found between the undulations, there
considered hills, until it was discovered that it
stretched for fifty miles in an almost direct line.
It thereupon received its baptismal name, which
was, after a little time, abbreviated into "Newfound," by which appellation it is, in the phrase
of the law, still called and known.

War and its effects have wrought a sorrowful
change in the old county, as in other sections of
the State. It lay right in the track of the armies,
and the civilization which existed there in the

old days before the war has perished almost as utterly as that of Nineveh or of Karnak. But at the time when the events herein related occurred, the country on Newfound was one of the old "neighborhoods" of the State. It was as retired and as quiet as one of the coves of Newfound Millpond where the waterlilies slept in a repose undisturbed by the outside current. Into this quiet life little excitement ever came from the outer world with which the chief connecting link was the sleepy mailrider who passed up the main road twice a week dropping his papers at the "big-gates" which were the outward signs of the plantations that lay secluded beyond the screening woods and leaving his letters at the Crossroads post-office. The excitement of that life was all supplied by the inhabitants themselves. Politics there meant how this or that or the other man cast his vote; religion was gauged by the spiritual experiences and conduct of this or that member, and civilization itself was weighed and tested by the life lived on the plantations. But even the events in their lives did not usually stir those denizens more than the breezes stirred the lily pads which, though moved a little on the surface, being anchored to the soil soon settled back in their accustomed places. The Landons and others of their kind ruled unquestioned in a sort of untitled manorial system; their poor neighbors stood in a peculiar relation to them, part friend, part retainer, the line between independence and vassalage being impalpable; and peace and plenty reigned over a smiling land.

The value of a plantation in those old times was largely determined by the amount of ''bottom-land'' on it, the uplands being poor, or, at least, having been worked out.

The finest ''bottom'' on Newfound was that at Landon Hall, which was, indeed, the only one distinguished by the more dignified name of ''low ground.'' Year in and year out it brought corn so ''rank'' that, in the picturesque language of the negroes, ''you just could follow the balk,'' by which was meant that one could just detect or follow with the eye the spaces between the rows.

Perhaps, it was this perennial abundance of the harvest which gave the Landons their prestige in the county quite as much as the fact that they held their lands under the same grant which had been issued by Charles II to the first of the name who had crossed the seas.

Father and son, for six generations they had

held it, and it was their boast that in all this period they had lost but one field.

This was the tract of a hundred acres or so of arable land, and a little more of marsh, beyond Newfound, which the fourth Landon had in very exuberance of recklessness lost one night at cards to a neighbor by the name of Bland. That side of Newfound was swampy, at best, from the backwater of the Landon mill-pond, and the tract was chiefly valuable because on it stood the quaint old gray frame-dwelling with its dormer windows and hipped roof, which the first Landon had built and named "Landon Hill," and in which they had lived until they erected the imposing mansion on the eminence on the other side of the stream, which they called "Landon Hall." His friend had badgered him to bet the land, and he had done so and lost. He offered to redeem it at twice its value; but the proposal was rejected. The friends became bitter enemies, and a duel had in time followed in which Landon had shot his adversary.

This, however, after the manner of most duels, had not remedied the matter.

It was found that the owner had the night before, with malignant prevision, executed a will leaving the land entailed as far as possible, and

6

with conditions which effectually prevented it
again passing into the hands of a Landon for at
least several generations.

From this time the old place was Naboth's
vineyard to the Landons. The house, peaked
and gray with age, stood on a rise across the low
grounds and the river immediately in front of
the lofty hill on which rose the Landons' com-
manding mansion. It was so situated that it
could not be shut out of the landscape. It was
the one place in sight from that eminence which
did not belong to the Landons, and it had been
the cradle of the race: of a race which prided itself on being an older branch than that which
remained in England, and on having brought its
landholding instincts across the water.

No wonder the Landons chafed and fretted
over its loss.

The son of the one who threw away the old
home retrieved the impaired fortunes of the
family by marrying an heiress, and the Landons
became wealthier than ever. Large offers were
made to the owner of the old place to repurchase
it; but the will of Bland, the duellist, effectually
prevented its recovery, and Colonel Landon
compensated himself and his wife by adding to
the estate on the other side, and rebuilding Lan-

don Hall in magnificent style. The limitation did not expire for two generations, and Colonel Landon left in his will a provision inculcating the necessity of securing the lost tract as soon as it was possible to do so. The colonel's son, who was Major Landon, on coming into the estate endeavored faithfully to fulfil his father's behest, and watched eagerly for the death of the old woman with whose life the limitations on the lost land expired. She lived in the far south, and the place for several years was unoccupied and neglected, the fences going down, the old, quaint, frame-house falling into disrepair, and the fields growing up in sassafras and pine until the entire farm became little better than a wilderness. As soon as Major Landon heard of her death he despatched an agent to the south to secure from the heir the option to purchase; but to his mortification and chagrin he found that the property had the day before he applied for it been sold. He immediately wrote and offered the purchaser, an old navy surgeon, one Dr. Browne, a handsome advance on his price; but it was declined on the ground that the doctor had bought it for a home and would not sell it at any figure whatsoever.

This almost threw the Major into a fever. To

be balked of what he had been reared to look forward to was like being defrauded of a part of his inheritance.

Shortly afterwards the old doctor arrived with his family, which consisted of a little granddaughter and two old negroes, one of whom was his body-servant, and the other the child's mammy.

Major Landon, after the custom of the country, called formally on the new neighbor; but he was not received, and it soon became known that the newcomer was not at home to visitors and wished to be let alone. This was as open a violation of the custom on Newfound as if the new settler had waylaid his neighbor from behind a fence, and from that time the aversion of the Major, and the suspicion of the rest of the community fell upon the new residents.

Stories soon began to be told of them and their "strange doin's": of how the old doctor used to prowl around the country at night, though he would not stir from his place by day— or at least, would not go on "the main, plain road"; but always stuck to by-paths; of how the two negroes were not like other black-folks, but talked sometimes a strange jargon and were in fact, "free niggers"; and of how a strange man

9

in black, used to come from town to have church
with them in some sort of a papist fashion. To
be sure there were those who said that the old
man was a mighty good doctor and though he
did not practise generally, was always ready
to go to a poor man's family and what was more,
never made any charge for it; and as to the
negroes, their talk was only a French patois and
the man in black who came was only a Catholic
priest from the City forty miles away. Still
there was nothing so remarkable as for a man
to differ so much from his neighbors as to shut
himself up. To refuse all hospitality he must
have something wrong about him. This was a
proposition which could not be questioned. In
time a word was whispered about concerning
him which could only be whispered: "Abolitionist."

Still there was no proof.

II

THEY were an austere people, the Landons,
reaping where they had not sown, and
gathering where they had not strewn. Tall,
straight, keen-eyed, aquiline they grew, father
and son, for generation after generation, as distinct from their plain neighbors on Newfound
as a Lombardy poplar is from the common pine.
The Major was the austerest of the race. He
reigned supreme on Newfound: a benevolent
tyrant with a tongue of flame, tempered happily
by a heart really kind at the core and easily
touched. His temper was explosive; but rarely
lasted longer than the first outburst and this
was generally followed by a period of calm and
kindness.

It was an accepted fact on Newfound that
every man, woman, and child gave way to the
Major except Bruce. Bruce was his only son.
and the prospective heir to the Landon Hall
plantation, with its four thousand acres and its
five hundred negroes.

As Bruce sprang up tall and slim, yet straight,

11

muscular and active, the resemblance between him and the Major, "the Landon favor," as it was called, was marked. There was in both the same finely cut face and clean figure, the same deep-set, clear gray eyes under strong brows, the slightly aquiline nose, the wide mouth full of fine teeth, and the firm chin and jaw, but more than this, was the resemblance in character. The same spirit discovered itself in each: an indomitable resolution to carry out his will which showed itself in every line of the face and every fibre of the frame. The Major was stern and imperative; the boy was resolute and defiant. "That boy is so like me sometimes that it frightens me," said the Major once to his wife, of whom happily, there was also something in her son. One of the servants expressed it once by the saying, "De chip don' fly fur from de stump." In truth, Bruce Landon was as like his father as it was possible to be, and this likeness did not stop at mere physical resemblance.

"He has the Landon bull-dog in him," said the Major, proudly; "he will not give up unless you kill him." If Mrs. Landon sighed over this particular tribute of praise, it was because she knew how the Landon obstinacy had too often brought sorrow to the Landons.

Once when Bruce was being thrashed for going fishing in disobedience to orders, he faced the Major, and looking him straight in the eyes said doggedly, "You 'd better give me two now; for I 'm going again." To the credit of the Major, it must be said, that this exhibition of the unconquerable will of the family for that time got the boy off.

By the time Bruce was thirteen he was almost as well known on Newfound as his father. At least twice he had been fished out of the millpond unconscious (once when he was pulled out by Dick Runaway, and once when he had got Dick out), besides any number of times when he had fallen in and been got out before he reached that state.

Sam Mills considered him a prodigy and Sam Mills was something of an oracle on Newfound, being given to observing changes, whether in men or weather. He always spoke of his qualities as if he had been a young puppy and possibly the similitude was nearer in some respects than Sam Mills meant to imply.

It was more than rumored that Bruce had once or twice met some of the runaway negroes who skulked around in the woods, and had hunted with them. The consorting with or having anything to do with this class of miscreants was at this time a high offense socially as well as legally. No one but Bruce could have stood this charge. Bruce did not deny it. He simply claimed that Dick Runaway, as he was called, was his father's negro, and no one had anything to do with it.

Dick was one of Major Landon's negroes and so incorrigible a runaway that he was known throughout the neighborhood and was by many of the neighbors considered a nuisance, if not a menace to the good order that prevailed. Some of Major Landon's friends had been inclined to take him to task for his leniency in the matter and had urged on him the duty of selling him and thus relieving the section of a bad example likely to spread and produce disastrous consequences. The Major, however, was not willing to sell any of his servants. He always regarded it as an act unbecoming a gentleman except under the spur of extreme necessity, and he was never given to accepting suggestions unless they chimed in with his own views.

Dick was a big black fellow of the pure South African type, with brawny muscles, white teeth, a big jaw and keen eyes. The love of liberty and the spirit of the jungle still gripped him so

14

fiercely that all steady work was as irksome to him as to an unbroken horse. Thus, even when he was at work he was so inclined to shirk it that he was constantly in trouble with Bailiff, the overseer. Punishment appeared to have little effect and if he was whipped he ran away. This had in time become almost a fixed habit with him and three or four times every year Dick was reported by the overseer to be missing. Sometimes, he would be caught and brought back by those who made it their business to apprehend runaways,—among whom was a certain "Pokeberry Green," whose chief occupation appeared to be hunting the runaways,—and sometimes he reappeared of his own accord and took uncomplainingly the modified punishment visited upon those delinquents who surrendered themselves and thus saved the cost of a reward. It is possible that Major Landon's patience might have given out but for an accident connected with one of Dick's escapades.

As Bruce grew to be a bigger boy he first shook off the trammels of his Mammy and then of the negro boy of about his own age who was selected to be his attendant and prepared to hunt and fish alone. His luck certainly appeared to be so much better as to justify him; but the fact was that Bruce had found a new comrade more to his taste. He was down on the river one day fishing when the bushes suddenly parted behind him and Dick made his appearance. He was clad very differently from the neat manner in which Major Landon's servants were usually clad. An old shirt, a pair of ragged trousers fastened at the waist with a leather strap, and an old straw hat were all he wore except a small strap knotted tightly about his wrist. At first Bruce was a little startled, for Dick was on one of his periodical escapades. But in a moment he was reassured, and that day was one of the most delightful in the boy's experience.

"Dis aint no place to fish," declared Dick scornfully. "You come with me and I'll show you whar fish is. I done bait de hole."

Bruce promptly rolled up his line and followed his guide, who instead of following the path struck at once into the swamp, picking his way, as Bruce observed, with wonderful skill through marshy places; at times wading in the water, at times treading on green hammocks till at length he brought Bruce into the deepest

16

recesses of the swamp. Here, after a little careful creeping through the brake, they came to a small wooded island which was swept on one side by the current and on another opened on a little cove completely screened by overhanging trees, under one of which lay an old skiff. Close by was Dick's favorite lair which he divulged to Bruce under a promise of the most absolute secrecy; a sort of booth formed of boughs and old boards. Here Dick was in reasonable security as he explained, "even from dat Pokeberry"; for his hounds could not track him there and even should they find him he could escape to the other side. Bruce expressed his detestation of Pokeberry. "I 'd a kilt him long ago," said Dick, "if I had 'n been feared dee 'd hang me. But some day he 's gwine to git drowndid."

"You are not going to drown him?" exclaimed the boy.

"Not a bit; de water gwine to do dat," said Dick oracularly "I 'm gwine to lead him whar he 'll wish he had n't gone, dat 's all, caze he can't swim."

Here, indeed, the fish bit as Bruce had never known them bite elsewhere. But better even

17

than that was the sport of having Dick light his fire and cook a dinner of fresh fish, "fat meat," and corn hoe-cake.

Bruce was so much pleased with his experience that one day a little later he determined to try his skill as a runaway and visit Dick in his island and had gotten nearly over the deep part when his foot slipped and down he went over his head. Unhappily his efforts carried him out into deeper water. He went down again choking and strangling and the Landon name might have ended then and there had not Dick Runaway happened to be near enough to plunge in and pull him out.

Even then Bruce was so far gone that Dick finding he was so very ill took him in his arms and braving whatever might befall himself rushed with him for home. Fortunately the Major was riding in the field which Dick had to cross and he met the terrified negro with his limp burden in his arms. Taking the boy up on his horse he galloped to his home where prompt remedies applied soon brought Bruce around. The boy's first inquiries were for Dick, and he would not be quiet until he had secured Dick's full pardon.

In fact, this act stood Dick in stead, not only

18

for that time; but for all future occasions when the spirit seized him and he took to the woods. The Major was forced to admit the overseer's charge that Dick was not only a shirker himself but set a disastrous example to the rest of the plantation. But as often as he thought of taking efficient steps to put a stop to Dick's vagrancy, the recollection of Bruce's white face as he lay limp and unconscious in Dick's big black arms that day intervened to defer all action.

There was only one person with whom Bruce Landon was not on good terms. This was the young man "Pokeberry Green" who had come to the neighborhood a few years before, drifted from no one knew where, though a strong accent and familiarity with the purlieus of a great city led to grave suspicion of his origin, which was subsequently verified. He had more education than most of the denizens and had evidently travelled both North and South. He was too lazy to engage in regular work, and lived generally by his wits. His only ostensible occupation was hunting. This he extended occasionally to hunting and now and then capturing such runaway negroes as might from time to time, for fancied or real grievances, leave their homes and take to the woods. A strange thing was, that although he was known to do this, he had appeared on better terms with the negroes than with the whites.

Once or twice he appeared to have large amounts of money, which he said had been left him, and which he had gone off to get. He soon ran through them, however. At other times he used to hang around the Crossroads "groggery," drinking whenever he could get whiskey. He was a heavy, muscular fellow, with stiff black hair, a red skin, and small, dark, hard eyes; a man of whom one would at once say the moral fibres were as coarse as a doormat. He was much hated by some of the negroes, and generally detested by the whites; but he possessed a certain shrewdness united to a deal of effrontery which made him feared if not popular with the lowest members of the lowest class. He called himself "Mr. Green," and a long, deep purple mark on the side of his heavy jaw and neck, which might have been a scar, but which he averred was a birthmark, had given him the name of "Pokeberry." Between this man and Bruce there was the deepest hatred, which neither pretended to conceal. Pokeberry was a born bully, and Bruce brooked no insolence. On one occasion when they met at Jones's Crossroads whither Bruce had gone to get the semi-weekly mail, their dislike flamed into a collision. Pokeberry, angered at some recent and caustic criticism of Major Landon's on his suspicious mode of life, had made some allusion to the story of the boy's meeting the runaway negroes and hunting with them. The boy to the enjoyment of the little audience gathered in the lazy afternoon about the post-office, retorted by calling him a "nigger-hunter." A fierce quarrel ensued, and Bruce had got much applause by suddenly attacking the bully and felling him to the ground with a stick which lay conveniently at hand. From this time they were sworn enemies.

As much credit, however, as Bruce gained from these things, his reputation on Newfound was based less on them than on his well-known resistance to his father. He was about the only person who dared to stand out against the major.

From this time the boy began to be counted as a rising scion of the Landon stock; for this was in the period before the war when courage and readiness to fight were reckoned among the most proper if not the most admirable traits of a man and were as much expected in him as if he had been a game-cock.

III

I T 'S becus they 's so high sperited," a thin
dim-looking fellow of about forty, dressed
in an old suit, of which the coat was much too
large for him, and the trousers much too small,
explained drawlingly one afternoon to a contem-
plative group around him at Jones's Crossroads, where the family traits of the Landons
were being discussed.

The speaker was Sam Mills. Sam was a great
friend of the Major's and was an authority.

"It 's becus they 's got so much of the devil
in 'em," declared Squire Johnson, burning at
the recollection of the scarcely veiled contempt
and the sharp-edged speeches with which the
major usually deigned to recognize his existence.
"Ef I ever git him befo' me, I 'm gwine to show
him who 's th' majistrit in this *district!*"

The squire was a large, burly man, with a
smooth-shaven red face, and a heavy bunch of
grizzled whisker growing under his large chin.

"Ef you does," said one of the bystanders, "you won' be majistrit long." He looked over towards Mills for corroboration.

The squire was turning to him when Mills intercepted him.

"You ain' never gwine to git him befo' you," he drawled; "he ain' got no use for law."

The justice turned his quid of tobacco over and over in his mouth, chewing with a force which attested the violence of his feelings. Mills understood the act as if it had been articulate speech.

"1 heard him say so myself," he asserted, as if he had been contradicted.

"What 'd he say?" a chewing individual on the fence, in brown jeans and an old straw hat, found the energy to inquire.

"He said he 'd 'a' had old Dr. Browne up for turning his cows into his corn long ago if th' had a jestice with any sense; but he ruther let the cows eat his corn than make a fool of himself going befo' a fool to try an' git jestice."

There was a gleam of satisfaction in the small gray eyes of the speaker as he glanced over at the man in the chair, and saw how his shafts had penetrated his armor of self-conceit. The individual referred to, whose mouth was too full to admit of an attempt to speak, chewed rancorously.

"He ain' never forgive me for goin' against him when he run for the Convention," he said, wiping the stained mouth on the palm of his hand.

"He ain' never forgive you for whippin' that nigger Dick of his whar you all caught out without a pass that night," said Mills, with the air of a man who knows the secret things. "He said you an' Pokeberry was the cusses of the county an' stirred up mo' trouble with the niggers 'n anything else."

The magistrate swore under his breath. Being classed with Pokeberry was more than he could stand.

"Ef I foun' a nigger roamin' aroun' without a pass, was I to change the law becus 'twas one of his niggers?" he said, in a complaining tone.

"He said 'twant the law; that the nigger give a good excuse: he told you he was gwine for th' doctor, and he was on a mule; and if you 'd 'a' had any sense you would 'a' knowed it. He said he don't allow nobody to touch one o' his niggers; and he said the law talks about discretion of them whar ain't got as much discretion as his horse."

24

"Them Landons is the hard feelin'est folks in Ameriky. They 's wuss 'n Injuns!" declared the dispenser of justice.

"Don' know 'bout that," drawled Mills; "but he cert'ny's got some 'n against you. I don' think you 'll git his endorsement next time."

This sally provoked a chuckle of amusement from the speaker and his auditors, which was so distasteful to the justice that he rose.

"I don' ixpect him and I don' want him," he declared, looking defiantly at his tormentors. "Ef I ever git him befo' me, I 'll show him who 's the jestice in this *district*."

He stalked over to where his lean horse stood tied to the fence, and prepared to leave.

"He says the squa'r don' know as much law as his horse," said Mills, in a confidential undertone. "He says if he had known what a fool he was, he 'd 'a' took the place himself ruther than have him saddled on the county."

"I 'd like to see the Major befo' him onct." hazarded his companion.

"You 'd see the ha'r fly," was Mills's reply.

"They are a curisome folks," he added meditatively, presently, after a pause during which the pompous old magistrate had mounted his dejected beast and ridden away. "Ain' a kinderhearteder man in th' worl' than the ole Major if you take him right; but you can't shove him, not a inch,—not a inch,'' he repeated.

A grunt of acquiescence from his companions reached him.

They were ruminant creatures, these quiet dwellers on Newfound; they chewed their straws, or tobacco and plodded along their accustomed way as placidly as oxen, but stirred out of their wonted calm they were as difficult to handle. Mills evidently did not expect any other answer, for he proceeded:

''When my ole ooman was took down that time, he comed over thar mo' reg'lar 'n th' doctor, and he knowed what to do for her jes' as good as him.''

The slanting sun fell through the trees on the little group in their coarse, rusty, old coats, and lit up their rugged faces.

''But if you stir 'im up, umph!'' (The inarticulate grunt expressed fully the speaker's views.) ''What you heard me tell the ole squa'r thar jes' now is the truth. He ain' never gwine forgive him. He ain' th' forgivin' kind. Ain' but two folks in th' worl' he don' like,—the squa'r an' ole Dr. Browne.''

''Three, you ought to say,'' interrupted one

of his friends, a short, wiry, sunburned, red-headed fellow named Hall, with a turned-up nose and a big mouth.—"An' Pokeberry. Thar he comes now."

"Yes, and Pokeberry," assented the other. "He said that he believed that Pokeberry is at the bottom of more than half the devilment the niggers cuts up, and he jist wisht he could prove it on him."

"You don't reckon there 's anything in that word about Pokeberry 's stealin' niggers, does you?" asked one of the group of the speaker. The reply was a grunt which might have been taken either way. It led to a general discussion of the suspicious circumstances in Pokeberry's career, each man contributing his quota until they had fabricated a fairly good case against that by no means immaculate individual.

The members of the group turned themselves lazily and glanced up the sandy road, down which, at a slouching pace, came a stout, heavy-set man of about thirty, with a gun thrown across his arm, and two thin, undersized, spotted hounds walking at his heel.

The contemplation of Pokeberry as he approached appeared to engross all the faculties of the little group against the fence, and they

27

chewed their tobacco in silence until he had turned in at the open door of the little store and disappeared from their view.

"Yes, an' Pokeberry," said Mills, taking up the thread just where he had left off. "He put him an' the squa'r together. He said he won't have him trackin' his niggers with houn's."

"Houn's cain't hurt nobody," drawled one of the group. "Houn's is the feardest dogs in the worl'."

" 'T aint that," explained Mills, with superiority. "He says, 't is the feelin'."

"I wonder the Major ain' never had the squa'r turned out?" said a man on the fence.

"Nor; he would n' put himself out enough to do that," explained Mills. "He knows the squa'r is po', and he won't take no step to take the office away from him."

"I b'lieve he 'd rather keep the squa'r in than to turn him out," suggested Hall, who had some sense of humor. "If he was to los' him, he would n' have nobody to abuse."

"He could abuse that tother ole man crost the river yonder where 's got his land," said Mills, with a sideways nod of his head to the smoky ridge away across the wooded bottom to the right, through which Newfound crept.

"That 's so," assented Hall, cordially. "Won-

der what makes the Major d'spise him so? Becus he would n' sell him the ole place?"

"Nor; becus he 's so curious; becus he won't
have nothin' 't all to do with nobody, and jes'
keeps himself shet up with them two ole niggers
an' that little gal o' his. They say, to be sure,
he 's mighty good to her—leastways, so the niggers says, and they knows everything."

"The Major says he ain' never been able to
lay eyes on him since he come heah an' settle
down on that place right crost the river from
him, where his fathers was born and raised, and
where by rights b'longest to him anyhow. He
says he shet himself up like a snake in his hole,
and he wisht he 'd shet his cows up too."

There was a gleam of amusement at the witti-
cism about the cows which was appreciated by
the plain farmer folk.

"Ain' never seen him in that time?" repeated
one or two. "Does look like something was
wrong."

"He said they say he 's a gentleman; but
he 'd like some proof of it. He never seen a
gentleman 's was afraid to look a man in the
face." Sam Mills liked to quote the Major. It
was like riding a better horse than his neighbor's. "He says he could n't be more secret if
he was an abolitionist."

29

This was enough in a neighborhood where every incident of every man's life was as well known and as freely canvassed by his neighbors as if it had happened to themselves. It was inexplicable except on the theory of either madness or crime, and, like more enlightened people, the dwellers on Newfound chose the less charitable theory. As, however, it was not the custom under that civilization for a man to interfere with any one else unless some personal act was committed which peculiarly affected him, the old recluse with his two attendants and his little grand-daughter was left unmolested in his pine-surrounded hermitage; and his wealthy neighbor contented himself with gibing at his singular seclusion, and with forbidding Bruce ever to extend his fishing or hunting excursions to the other side of the little river, or even to go on his land.

The coolness with which Bruce disobeyed him incensed him. It had been amusing enough while he was a little tot to laugh at his defiant airs, but the time had come to pull him up short. Even Mrs. Landon with all her mildness and though her tender heart was wrung could not but admit that for this time Bruce was in the wrong.

IV

WHETHER it was that the best fishing-holes were on Dr. Browne's side of the river, and that the river-duck especially loved the "collard"-filled cove with its succulent grasses which the backwater from the Major's mill-pond made on that bank, or whether it was Bruce's natural and inevitable propensity to do that which was forbidden, the boy very shortly disobeyed his father's injunction. He came home one day with a fine string of fish which he boldly announced that he and Dick had caught on Dr. Browne's bank.

The Major was immediately in a passion. He declared that Bruce had ruined Dick and made him a runaway, and wound up by demanding that the boy should with his own hands immediately take the fish straight back to their owner.

Bruce refused.

There was a pitched battle, in which the Major gave Bruce, as usual, a tremendous thrashing;

31

but received still the same dogged reply he had made him from the first, "I won't do it if you kill me." Then he ordered him to bed.

The boy went, though it was early in the afternoon.

Then his mother, who always acted the peacemaker between the two, went up-stairs to him.

Bruce was lying in bed, looking longingly out of the window. His eyes had an angry gleam in them, and his mouth was drawn. It is not far, however, from a mother's heart to her son's, and in a few moments the boy was weeping in his mother's arms. Her tenderness brought the submission which the Major's discipline had failed to secure. Sitting on the bed by the boy, holding his hand in both of hers, she told him a story.

It was that long years before when his father was a boy just his age, he had had an elder brother named Bruce. He was wilful and disobedient; defied all authority. One day his father, angered by his insubordination, in a passion said to him that he was a disgrace to the name he bore. "Then I will never disgrace it any more," he said angrily; "for I never will bear it again," and with that he had rushed out of the house and disappeared. The next day his hat was found

32

floating on the pond. The dam was cut, the river was dragged, and every effort was made to recover the body, but in vain. It killed his mother, and embittered his father's whole after-life. He never got over it.

Mrs. Landon broke down, weeping at the thought of the sad, bereft mother. She leaned over and drew her son to her bosom, and kissed him again and again.

"O Bruce, Bruce! my son! my son!" she sobbed.

In a little while Bruce came down and said he would take the fish back. He, however, announced boldly that he was going because his mother wished him to go, and thought that he ought not to catch fish on another's land without permission, and not because he had been whipped.

The boy's feelings as, after he crossed the river, he rode his colt along the old road through the pines were so strange and so complex that he remembered them years afterwards. It was the first time he had ever been on the place, and he had never seen any one who had been there except Dick Runaway.

The shame he felt as he rode along at having to confess that he had caught the fish on an-

other's property without permission gave way
to a feeling of curiosity as he came in sight of
the dense hedge of cedars which surrounded the
yard as with a wall. The pines grew up almost
to the hedge. He passed between two old leaning gate-posts from one of which hung the
broken fragment of an ancient gate, and found
himself in a yard all grown up in weeds and
bushes, except on one side where there was a
flower garden. Just before him was a long, low,
weather-stained frame-dwelling with a hipped
roof, queer wings, and quaint dormer windows
jutting out.

Bruce rode up, and stopped in front of the
door. As no one appeared, he called,

"Hello!"

From an old and ruinous out-building came
back, "Hello!" but there was no one in sight.

"Hello!" he called again, and again came the
short reply, "Hello!" which he found was
nothing but an echo from the old building at the
side.

After waiting a moment, he decided that he
could not have been seen, and rode on and tied
his horse to an overhanging limb, and went up
to the door.

He knocked. The stillness was so intense that

the sound of his rapping made him jump. The odours of the locust blossoms became oppressive and the hum of the bees among them filled all the silence. He was about to leave and go around to the other side of the house, when a door opened at the far end of the passage, and an elderly negro woman, thin and black, and with her head tied up in a blue checked handkerchief, appeared and came slowly towards him.

"Good evening," said Bruce, and then, without waiting for her to speak, began rapidly:

"Here is a string of fish I caught down yonder on your side of the pond, and my mother sent me to bring them back." He paused to swallow, for his throat was dry.

"Who you say sent 'em?" asked the woman, looking at them curiously.

"My mother,—my father—Major Landon. I caught them."

The woman's face brightened.

"Thankee, little marster," she said.

The boy saw that she considered them a present. The temptation was strong to leave her under the impression; for he had told her once why he had brought them back; but Bruce was as honest as day. A Landon would not lie. He thought of that saying of Brian de Bois Guilbert, "Many a law and many a commandment have I broken; but my word never," and he gulped out,

"They are not a present—I caught them on this side,—on your side, and my mother—and my father—sent them back: my father is Major Landon."

"What 's all this?" inquired a stern voice.

Bruce turned in amazement at the sound of the voice. An old gentleman, tall and gray, stood behind him.

"What was that you were saying?" he asked sharply, his keen dark eyes gleaming from beneath his shaggy, white eyebrows. The stern voice and the flash of the deep eyes above the eagle-like nose seemed so familiar to the boy, that he insensibly assumed a hostile attitude. But he went through his formula honestly.

"I caught some fish on your side of the river, and I have brought them back, as my mother and father thought I ought not to have done it without permission."

The sturdy honesty of the boy and the evident struggle he underwent attracted the old man, and a kindly light stole into his eyes.

"So you caught them without permission, did you, and they made you bring them back?"

A curious look shone even through his long beard.

"I brought them because my mother wanted me to do it," said Bruce doggedly.

"Oh, because your mother wanted it?" he muttered. He had averted his face slightly, but now he turned to the boy, and laying his hand on his head, he said gently,

"You have my permission to fish or hunt, or do anything you wish anywhere on my property; but, my son, remember this, 'Honor thy father and thy mother, that thy days may be long in the land which the Lord thy God giveth thee.' " He suddenly turned and walked into the house.

When Bruce came home that night he avowed himself the friend of his new acquaintance, and from that time he was his steadfast champion.

He gave notice of the permission he had received, and boldly announced his purpose to avail himself of it. There was another battle which might be said to have been drawn, as neither side was conquered, and each stood at the end just where he stood at the beginning of the contest.

It was not very long afterwards that he carried out his purpose, and crossing the pond went over to the forbidden bank. The ducks he was after, however, were not found, having been probably frightened off by the cows that were grazing down in the marsh, and whose bells he heard mellowed in the distance. He followed a narrow path which led along the edge of a little inlet filled with tasselled alder bushes. Up at its further point inland a fine spring bubbled from beneath a flat rock above which towered a poplar, straight and clean of limb for fifty feet. Another path came down the hill to the spring from the woods above. The water from the spring for some distance ran down rippling over a bed of clean sand just beside the path and then turned away into the thickets of alders.

Bruce, laying his gun down, stooped and drank at the spring, and then flung himself on the ground at the foot of the poplar, and fixing his head comfortably, gazed up at the blue summer sky. He heard the faint clatter of the cowbells below him, softened by the distance to a low, mellow, and irregular tinkle. He heard the water purling over some pebbles close by; he heard a woodwren's bright note in a tree above; he heard the faint call of his father's ploughmen across the pond to their teams, and then—he felt a hand or something on his face, and then— some one kissed him; and, opening his eyes, he found himself looking up into the wide-open, and somewhat startled big brown eyes of a little girl who was kneeling beside him, bending over him with a look of mingled wonderment and pleasure. Her cheeks were as pink as roses, and her curling hair was hanging in tangles on either side of her throat, leaving her oval face like a picture set in a frame of loosely twisted dull red gold.

As Bruce opened his eyes, she drew back with a start.

"Oh, it 's come true!" she exclaimed with a little gasp, throwing herself back and sitting on her feet, and clasping her small hands tightly in her excitement. Her great dark eyes were dancing in her head.

The child was so pretty that the boy lay still with his eyes on her, fearing that a motion might frighten her.

"What has come true?" he asked presently.

"What grandpapa and mammy read me out of the fairy book," she said, throwing her hair back out of her way.

"What was that?"

"Why, about the prince who came down out of the sky (but he was asleep), and the princess that kissed him, and waked him up, and made

39

him love her, and they lived happily together all their lives."

"Oh! about that!" said Bruce, definitely.

"Are n't you the prince?" she asked sweetly, moved by a faint suspicion at something in his voice.

"You are the princess, at any rate," said the boy, gallantly, raising himself on his elbow and looking at her with admiration.

"No, I 'm not the princess; I 'm nothing but a little girl; but when I found you here I knew you were the prince, and I thought it might do even if I were not the princess, and I do want somebody to play with so bad." The little face was quite pitiful.

"Grandpapa an' mammy an' Unc' Polium an' Laz'rus and George Washington do all they can; but I want a prince. Are n't you a prince, sure enough?" She asked the question with a sudden return of faith, struck, perhaps, by the smile which lit up the handsome face of her companion.

"Well, they don't have many princes around here," said Bruce, evasively, and then a sudden thought struck him. "I will play that I am your prince."

"Oh, will you? And you will love me and play with me?"

She leant forward, and in her earnestness put one little plump, brown hand on the back of Bruce's. It thrilled him, boy as he was, with a sudden sense of ownership and protection.

"Yes," he nodded.

"And you will be good to Laz'rus and George Washington?"

Bruce nodded affirmatively; then inquired:

"Who are they?"

"Why, they are my cats, and they both have kittens."

"Have they?" exclaimed Bruce, in unfeigned surprise at this astonishing information.

She nodded.

"Umh—umh—!"

"What is your name, Prince?" she asked presently.

"Bruce."

"Oh, I know:—Bruce, prince of Scotland. Grandpapa told me about him. I'm so glad! I was afraid maybe you were an Eastern prince."

"No," said Bruce; "I am not one of those. Do you think I look like one?"

"Well, you must be mighty rich." She gazed

at his watch-chain with a look of appraisement; "but they wear chewnics, and are black like Unc' Polium."

"Who is Unc' Polium?" asked Bruce.

"Unc' Polium? don't you know him? He 's my mammy's husband, and my grandpapa's body-servant."

"Who is your grandpapa?"

"Grandpapa! Oh, he don't know grandpapa," she laughed in glee. "Well, how funny! Why, he 's my grandpapa,—my grandfather, you know," she explained.

"What 's his name?"

"What 's his name? Why, he has n't got any name—he 's just grandpapa, so. Oh, yes; mammy and Unc' Polium call him Master. I reckon that must be his name."

"No, that is n't a name at all," urged Bruce; "they call him that because they are slaves."

"They are n't slaves! My mammy ain't any slave!" exclaimed the child.

"Oh, ain't she? Where do you live?" he asked.

"Up there, at home." She pointed up the path.

The cow-bells sounded more distinctly, as the

cows passed up the hill. She rose and brushed the leaves and small sticks from her dress.

"It 's getting late; I must go. I hear Teensey going home; mammy's got her. Will you come with me?"

"No, I must go home," said Bruce.

"Well, will you come again to-morrow?"

"Yes; good evening."

"Good evening, Prince Bruce."—She put up her mouth to be kissed, and the boy stooped and kissed her gently.

"Run away, and I will wait until you are at the top of the hill," he said coaxingly. She started, and then stopped.

"Will you play with me?" she asked, turning and looking back at him.

"Yes; run along."

"And you will come back to-morrow?"

"Yes; to-morrow afternoon."

"Yes; when mammy comes after the cows?"

"Yes."

"Good by." And she ran up the hill, her little bare legs shining, and her loose hair streaming behind her.

43

V

WHEN Bruce reached home that evening he gave so graphic a description of his meeting with the little girl that his father was too much interested to upbraid him with his disobedience, and his mother was outspoken in her sympathy.

"What was her name?" she asked.

"I did n't think to ask her," Bruce replied.

"What, sir! Kiss a girl, and not know who she is?" said his father.

"She was mighty pretty," responded the boy, naïvely.

"Oh, she was? The name then does n't make so much difference," laughed his father.

"Oh, yes! her name is Margaret Reid," said Bruce. "Sam Mills told me so once."

The next afternoon Bruce was true to his appointment; but when he arrived at the spring, his little friend was not there. After waiting what, in his boyish impatience, appeared to him an age, he started up the path which led up the hill. Just before reaching the top, however, he heard a coaxing voice calling, "Kitty, Kitty, Kitty! Come along, Kitty!" and through the woods at a little distance appeared his little girl. Her head was bare, and she was carrying something in her large poke bonnet, the edges of which she was with much pains keeping together, whilst behind her, with tails erect, walked two cats, mewing and looking up at her.

At sight of Bruce she smiled and quickened her pace.

"Oh, have you come?" she called in a pleased tone. "I was late because George Washington would n't come, and King Alfred got under the porch and spit at me.—Get back there!" This was to a kitten whose little black head was protruding from the bonnet.

"Which is George Washington?" asked Bruce.

"That 's she, with the white nose. And King Alfred is her kitten. Here they are." And she suddenly let go one side of the calico bonnet and poured out on the ground a half-dozen kittens, on which the two cats immediately pounced with maternal solicitude.

"King Alfred will never go to heaven," she said suddenly, with that serious manner which characterized her utterances.

"Why, cats don't go to heaven," said Bruce.

"Oh, they do!"

"Where did you get that idea?"

"Why, grandpapa says that everything that loves goes to heaven; that Heaven is love."

This was a little too abstruse for the boy; but he saw that it would grieve her to disturb her belief, so he asked,

"What makes you think that King Alfred won't go to heaven?"

"Because he does n't mind what is said to him."

"Does that keep people from going to heaven?"

"Yes; grandpapa says that it 's the aw-fulest thing there is."

In his heart Bruce trusted that that particular sin did not shut the gates of mercy beyond hope; but he said nothing.

"Who is your mamma?" he asked presently.

"She is in heaven," said the child, simply.

"Who is your papa?"

"Papa is there too. He was a soldier."

There was a pause in which she was manifestly reflecting.

"Banquo is there too," she said presently.

"Who is he?" inquired Bruce, with a dim recollection of having read of some one of that name, but he could not recall where.

"He 's grandpapa's old dog."

"It seems to be a very large place," he suggested.

"It is," she said with quiet serenity.

By this time they had reached the spring, and the kittens were allowed a second release from their confinement in the bonnet.

"I told grandpapa about you," she said presently.

"You did? What did he say?"

"He said that you were not a prince at all."

"Did he say that?"

"Yes; and he said that I was a princess in his eyes." She seated herself on the ground beside Bruce, and leaned her elbow on his knee with perfect confidingness.

"And he said that you had better not come up there—up home." She waved her little hand up towards the top of the hill.

"Ah!"

"Yes; because your father would not like it."

A guilty feeling came over the boy, and he felt a longing to leave her under the belief in his innocence; but he said resolutely,

"He would n't."

47

"Why would n't he like it?" she asked, with the calm persistence of childhood.

"I don't know; he does n't like a good many things I do."

"Oh, does n't he? I do."

The unaffected praise of the child was very grateful to the boy, and a smile of pleasure came over his handsome face.

"I wish we could live together, don't you?" she said, suddenly turning and nestling up against him with perfect trustfulness.

The confidingness of the act was so sweet that the boy stooped over and kissed her gently.

"I wish we could," he said.

"We can get married, and I 'll give you my kitties, and you can have my mammy and grandpapa."

"All right," said Bruce, laughing at her seriousness.

"All right. I told grandpapa last night we were going to be married."

"You did? What did he say?"

"At first he laughed, and then he took me up on his knee and told me I did not know what I was talking about. And he said that when I grew up you would 'spise me, and that I would hate you; and then he got up and walked about and looked so angry I had to climb up on the chair and kiss him, and tell him I would not marry anybody but him.''

She had grown eloquent as she narrated the interview, and the boy thought she looked like a fairy, as she stood there instinctively imitating her grandfather's angry gestures. When she had ended she sank down beside him again.

''You won't 'spise me, will you?'' she asked pleadingly.

''No, that I won't,'' said Bruce, sincerely.

''And you will play with me, won't you? because I did wake you up, did n't I?''

''Yes. And you won't ever hate me?''

''No; and here 's my ring; it 's mine; and you must keep it just like we were married, and— there 's mammy calling me, and I must go.— Come here, kitties!''

She made a rush upon the kittens, which were drowsily taking their suppers, and gathering them up tossed them into her bonnet without much reference to their comfort, and with a hasty ''Good by,'' ran up the hill, hugging her precious burden to her bosom, and followed by the faithful Lazarus and George Washington mewing faintly.

That evening Bruce's recital was not received

by his father with the same complacency which he had exhibited the evening before.

"I thought I told you not to go over there again?" said he, sternly.

"You did not tell me so yesterday," asserted the boy.

"Did not tell you so yesterday? Do you think, sir, that I have nothing else to do but to spend my time telling you the same thing?"

He paused for a moment's reflection; then he said,

"Bruce, I want you to promise me not to go over there again."

The boy was silent; but the dogged look settled on his face. His father noted it.

"I should think you 'd be ashamed to associate with such people. They are low, and worthless, and unfit associates for a gentleman," he said sneeringly.

An angry light came into the boy's eyes. "They are not," he said.

"Don't contradict me, sir. They may be very fit associates for you if you have a taste for such companions; but they are nothing but common people. That little girl is the daughter of a low, common man like—Pokeberry Green, or his associates." He selected his shaft carefully.

"She is not," contradicted the boy, defiantly. "She is as much a lady—as—as any one,—and I will go there. And I will marry her when I grow up, and am a man." He stood before his father, with flashing eyes and fearless mien.

"Go to your room, sir," said the major in high wrath.

Bruce left the library and went up-stairs to his room; but his determination was unchanged.

The next day he learned that he was to be sent off to school at once, and that afternoon he was driven away in the carriage on his way to a school in another State.

VI

BRUCE LANDON remained from home the best part of eight years. The Major determined to give him not only the best education, but the advantages of travel as well. He meant if possible to eradicate the taste he thought he had discovered in him by broadening his mind. Bruce, having applied himself, easily won enough honors to satisfy even his father's ambition. The Landons had been noted of old for their distinction at William and Mary, and Bruce's successes awakened all his father's pride. On the few occasions when Bruce was at home from college the relations between them were, therefore, completely altered.

During this period affairs on Newfound remained in their wonted condition. Eight years made little difference in that quiet life. If affairs moved at all, they moved so slowly that a longer arc than eight years was needed to detect it. The pines had grown closer about Landon Hill, where the recluse doctor still kept himself shut up. The Major still gazed at the old place across the low grounds, and still cherished a negative kind of animosity against his neighbor, declaiming with much rancor of expression against the iniquity of his remaining secluded and allowing his cows to run on other people. Mills and Hall and other dwellers on the river still absorbed and reflected mildly the major's opinions. Squire Johnson, unmolested, still held his little office, contenting himself with an assertion of independence behind the Major's back. And Newfound still crept lazily between its low wood- or corn-covered banks, moving, like the people who lived upon it, slow, calm, sleepy.

What passed within the pine-girt hermitage where Dr. Browne lived with his grand-daughter and two old domestics no one outside knew.

The little negro man with his quaint old faded and patched uniform, his worn beaver, and his exaggerated manner, occasionally paid a visit to the mill for a small bag of meal or flour, or to the post-office to inquire for a letter, and except for these they held no more communication with the outer world than if they had been imprisoned in a dungeon.

Suspicion, fostered by Pokeberry Green, centred upon the old recluse with rather more definiteness than before. It was believed that in some way he was connected with the occasional disappearance of negroes in that region. It seemed to have a little more foundation. Pokeberry still followed his ungracious calling of trying to recapture runaway negroes. He had received another legacy which he had quickly squandered. Once or twice Pokeberry had started a report that Dr. Browne gave aid and comfort to the runaways; but it had died out. Had any one else but this man circulated such a report it would have been sufficient to have occasioned an investigation, if not to have driven the old man from the county. Had there not been the overwhelming circumstances of the doctor's suspicious conduct, Pokeberry's character was so bad that nothing he said could have had any weight. As it was, the two together were just sufficient to keep gossip alive about the owner of the old Landon place, and to make him and everything connected with him a matter of keen interest.

The eight years wrought more changes in the doctor's grand-daughter than in almost any one else on Newfound. The little girl that had found the prince under the poplar tree beside the spring grew up among the pines; her companions: her grandfather, her mammy, the progeny of Lazarus and George Washington, the roses and hollyhocks in the ancient tangled garden, and the friends she found in the few old volumes in the bookcase. They were a curious lot: Evelina, Clarissa Harlowe, Sir Charles Grandison, Pamela, Sir Roger de Coverley, Lord Orville, Lizzie Bennet, Mr. Darcy, Emma Woodhouse, and a few others besides the characters from the dramas of Corneille, Racine and Molière, and other French classics. Her grandfather was a great sufferer from an old wound, a confirmed invalid, and was often confined to his room and chair. But he taught her, though in a desultory way, enough to have made her quite the equal in education of most young ladies of her time, and as she had always spoken French she was soon more familiar with the classic French literature than with the English.

An invalid is next to a child in developing a woman's instincts. She read to him, tended him, and petted him as if he were a baby.

Once or twice she ventured, when a young girl, to accompany her mammy to the Crossroads store to make a few little purchases; but some tipsy men, one of whom had a long, ugly, purple scar on his sunburned cheek and neck, stared so at the straight, handsome, half-grown girl with her large brown eyes under her coarse hat, that she never again went beyond the pines in which was her world. Twice she met the same man with the purple scar, down on the pond. He came upon her each time as she was fishing. He tried to talk to her; but she hastily left the pond and ran home. The last time, he said something to her which she felt was impertinent, and she ever afterwards avoided that part of the pond.

Pokeberry, at the grocery, had drunkenly declared his admiration, and duly declared there, subsequently, his repulse.

One day she discovered up-stairs in the dark little garret several old trunks covered with dust and cobwebs. She opened one of them and found it filled with old dresses, and odds and ends of woman's wear, all curious, but rich and with the faint odors of lavender and long past summers in their folds. They must have been nearly a hundred years old. Some were lawns, filmy and faded as if with age, others stiff brocades with long waists and padded petticoats and stomachers. They made her eyes open.

Whom could they have belonged to?

She took them out tenderly and turned them

over and over with caressing hands; measured them by her own straight, supple figure, and in her fancy pictured them as belonging to the fine ladies she knew in the brown calf-backed books down-stairs. From this she began to dream of a later time. They must have belonged to some ancestors and she wondered how she herself would have looked in some of them. She ventured to ask her grandfather about them. He seemed startled and desired her not to go into the trunks. Her grandfather's wish was law to her, and she went no more for a long time. One day, however, she asked him about her mother. He became too agitated to tell her a great deal, except that she had died when she, Margaret, was born. Margaret knew that her father had been killed in a battle. And this was all she knew of her father or mother except that when she asked her mammy what she was like she always told her, "Like you, honey; jes' your size an' all, only prettier."

So she passed her time growing up, with her large eyes, and her sunny hair, tending her grandfather as he sat in his old arm-chair; living with her friends in the age-browned books; fishing in the pond; wandering in the pines; going after the cows; tending, because they were pretty, her hollyhocks, sweet-peas, and roses in the garden, as wild, yet as much at home among them, as the sparrows and thrushes which built in the lilacs.

If, as she ran wild about the place, or followed the paths through the pines in her search for the vagrant cows, she sometimes glanced over across the placid pond and the alder thickets to the green low-grounds and fields of Landon Hall, and may have felt a mild surmise as to the boy whom she had once found asleep under the tree by the spring, it was simply an act of memory, and the feeling was too vague to take definite shape.

In her isolated life Margaret Reid often found occasion to contemplate the difference between her situation and that of other girls of her age and condition. She had no friends except her grandfather and the old servants, and no companions except these and the few domestic animals they owned. Her situation cut her off from others of her age and kind about her as completely as though she had been an Eastern princess condemned to perpetual seclusion. She knew from her reading, and perhaps she felt in her heart that this was not natural, that there must be some compelling motive

58

which caused her grandfather to cut himself off from everyone about him, and though it never occurred to her to question the soundness of his position, yet she often wondered why he lived in such retirement. She knew that girls of her class were usually educated in convents, but there they made friends and had the guidance of the good sisters. And sometimes, she longed for the unknown, but imagined companionship of those of her own age. There were many young people in the neighborhood and with some of them she had formed a casual acquaintance; but though she liked them she was both shy and proud. Her grandfather held himself aloof from everyone, and she knew that in some way he was generally regarded with coldness. In her childhood she thought it might have been the difference in their religion, but as she grew older this idea waned. She asked Father Shannon something about it once; but the good father either did not know or felt it better not to enlighten her; so all she got was a pat on the head and a reply that her grandfather was the proper person to consult.

This naturally threw her back on herself and her face often wore a meditative expression which might have seemed melancholy had it not been so lovely in its soft dreaminess. This was the more charming because the sudden flash of her smile as her countenance lit up was like the sunlight breaking through a soft mist. Her whole expression became transformed. Yet, in this solitary life she found much that escapes those who rush headlong and heedless through existence. She came to know the wild things of wood and field as only those can know them who have a love for them and time in which to show it. Further, though she knew few people she knew much of those few. What puzzled her was the unequalled distribution of Nature's gifts: how some could have so much and some so little. When she spoke to her grandfather about this he gave her reasons which did not satisfy her: the established order: legal rights: the fact that the rich were not happier than the poor. She could not accept these views. It seemed to her that Mrs. Landon in her fine carriage with rustling silks must be happier than the drawling-voiced, slatternly women she saw in their cabins with their frowsy heads and dingy calico frocks. She felt so strongly about this that she determined to do what she could to alleviate the condition of these latter, and with this intention she went around among some of the poor neighbors

60

and offered to teach their children. When she consulted her grandfather he appeared amused at the idea. They did not want to be taught, he told her, and would not thank her for her pains. But she was so eager to try her project that he permitted her to make the trial. To her surprise, her offer was received with some suspicion and entire indifference. Even when under her perseverance they yielded a reluctant assent, it was evident that they considered it a favor to her.

In the years that had passed, Dick Runaway's hatred of Pokeberry Green had largely increased. Pokeberry was in the main unpopular enough with the dwellers on Newfound, white and black; but there were a few who whether they liked him or not were fain to put up with him, and among these was Runaway Dick. It was a high crime and misdemeanor to sell liquor to negroes and only those bold enough to defy or sharp enough to evade the law ventured to do so. But Pokeberry cared little for law, provided his infractions of it were not discovered. And as the runaway was very fond of liquor a sort of friendship at one time sprang up between the two men. Thus, Dick's lair which he had arranged with great shrewdness in the most inaccessible part of the swamp on Newfound was known to Pokeberry. He from time to time visited Dick there, having discovered the retreat through the slave's liking for his illicit ware. His visits he made in a boat which he handled with great skill, though curiously enough he could not swim a stroke. If the truth were known, Pokeberry in the beginning had had something to do with Dick's intermittent escapades, and these at first were largely due to Green's wily suggestions of the joys of freedom, especially when tinged with liberal draughts of whiskey. These eventually were carried further until Pokeberry began to tempt the runaway with undisguised promises of permanent freedom. There were times when Dick appeared to lend a willing ear to these alluring temptations, when, stretched on the grassy bank in the spring sunshine, he idly watched his corks floating on the placid surface of his choice fishing-holes and reflected how much pleasanter was a life of freedom than one of toil; or when, as sometimes happened, Pokeberry plied him with a fiery liquid from a stone jug which lay in his boat hidden among the reeds. Then, indeed, the breath of far-off African jungles seemed to breathe about the stalwart young

negro and savage instincts which had been
growing dormant for generations began to stir
within his breast, while the man with the deep
scar in his throat sat before him and with keen,
hard, cold eyes painted his wrongs and woes.
Once or twice Dick had almost yielded; but
when the morning came the toilsomeness of the
long journey which Pokeberry had painted as
necessary, made him pause and the memory of
the old plantation with its joys held him back.
There was one other thing. Pokeberry had
suggested that it might—indeed would be
necessary for Dick to pass himself off as his
slave. This degradation sank deep in Dick's
mind. Like the other servants at Landon Hall
he had always prided himself on belonging to a
gentleman. The shame of passing himself off
as belonging to one who not only was not of the
quality, but was actually the most despised man
in his region, staggered him. So although again
and again he appeared to Pokeberry on the eve
of assenting, as often as the time came for
their departure Dick refused. Finally came the
rupture. A story came back to the negroes
of the neighborhood that one of the men whom
Pokeberry claimed to have helped to freedom
was working in the far South in a far worse

slavery than he had ever known in his old home. When Pokeberry insisted on Dick's standing up to his agreement and threatened him with betrayal of his hiding place, Dick in return threatened to give himself up voluntarily and tell what Pokeberry had held out to him. There was a furious quarrel with Pokeberry gripping his gun hard with an ugly look in his eyes. Presently, however, he quailed and with a laugh began to curse Dick in a jocular tone for being such a fool as to take his words seriously. The quarrel was patched up by means of a fresh jug of liquor from Pokeberry's boat and the night ended with Dick in a stupor.

When Dick came to he was lying fast bound in a little covered wagon, into which were peering a number of curious faces. Pokeberry was talking to some one on the roadside. "He was jest gettin' ready to cut out when I got him and fact is I had to make him think I was helpin' him off to get him at all."

"You must a wasted a jag o' good liquor on him," said some one of the bystanders.

"Oh, I knew how to get him. 'There 's more ways of killin' a dog than chokin' him to death.' You can get some one way an' some another, but most of 'em tumbles to liquor."

"Specially to yours, Pokeberry," observed one of the others, at which there was a laugh and Pokeberry growled, and started his thin horse, while Dick swore vengeance against him in his heart.

They had not proceeded very far when the cart stopped and Pokeberry accosted some one.

"Good evenin' Miss. How 's yo' grandpa?"

"Very well, thank you," said a voice which, notwithstanding its coldness, Dick recognized as that of Dr. Browne's grand-daughter. She was about to pass on, but Pokeberry was barring her way in the road.

"You 'll be glad to know I 've caught that runaway nigger 't 's always hanging around the pond down yonder. I got him here in my cart, takin' him home, where he 'll git a good dressin' down."

Curiosity and pity combined at the cruel speech and Dick was conscious that a head leant forward and a pair of eyes different from any that had fallen on him that day rested on him. As the girl caught sight of the cords on Dick's wrists and ankles she wheeled suddenly on the driver, her timidity all vanished.

"You brute! How can you be so cruel! Do

you not see he is suffering? Untie him instantly or I myself will do it.''

Pokeberry laughed hoarsely, ''I 'm a brute, am I? Sufferin', is he? You think so? Wait till they sell him down South on one of them sugar plantations where you come from, then he 'll know what sufferin' is. You ask your grandpa. He can tell you about it.''

''Oh! don't you see how that rope is cutting his writs? Look how his hands are swollen. Loosen them, I say. Set him free.'' She spoke imperatively, but Pokeberry knew his hour of triumph.

''That 's right. That 's the way your grandpa would talk. He 's always for settin' 'em free. But I 'm a respectable citizen. I ain't any abolitionist and I 'll show 'em now. If he don't lay still in there I 'll tie him tight sure 'nough. Well, so long. I 'll keep you informed how your friend gits on. Git up.'' He gave his horse a cut with his switch and started on again with a mocking laugh, leaving the young girl standing in the road a picture of helpless sympathy and baffled indignation. But though the runaway's hands and feet were swollen they did not hurt him so much. That look of pity and those warm words of compassion had been a balm to his wounded spirit which had dragged the pain from his limbs and racked head. And though as the cart toiled on down the sandy roads the tears stole from under his tightly shut lids, they were rather the tears of self-compassion than of suffering, and he blessed the young Samaritan in his heart as much as he cursed his betrayer and captor.

One other thing added to his misery. He had to face the shame of being driven up to the overseer's house near the quarters, tied. He foresaw the public triumph of his enemy, the curiosity of his friends, and saw himself an object of their amusement and ridicule. He knew that there were many who would be glad of his humiliation—who had not the courage to run away and were quite content with their lot, which, indeed, to him, bound like a calf and driven towards an unknown fate, suddenly appeared as tranquil and blessed as Heaven. In his self pity he hoped he would die before he reached home with its curious eyes and contemptuous giggles over his misfortune and he vaguely tried to think how he might kill himself; but as the cart turned in at the plantation gate and began to make its way slowly across the wide field, his tension relaxed and he fell into an uneasy doze.

He was aroused by hearing his master's voice. "What 's that? You have caught my runaway negro? Very well. Where did you get him? He 's a trifling scoundrel—I shall have to sell him, I expect. How is he? He 's not sick, I hope?"

"No, s'r. He 's all right. I got him last night—been layin' for him a long time. He was gittin' ready to try to git off to New York or Philidelphy—that 's the way I got him."

Dick made a convulsive movement to sit up and denounce the liar, but he was too slow.

"What! Run off to the North! Well, I 'll just get rid of him—I 'll send him to New Orleans; better than New York or Philadelphia, anyhow, for, at least, he 'll get enough to eat and won't freeze to death."

Dick's eyes shut tight with a sudden spasm. He was glad he had not looked at his master.

"Why, where did that boy learn of those towns!" exclaimed the Major, after a second's reflection. "I did not know that he knew there were any such places in the world."

Pokeberry was ready.

"Well, they 's one way: your neighbor yonder 's owns part of your old place. I guess he knows about Philadelphia an' New York and Boston, too.

"That 's true. He 's a perfect pest. I wish we could get rid of him. He 'll have every thing by the ears here if he stays much longer. Well, take that rascal to the house and turn him over to the overseer.

"Yes, s'r, and he 'll attend to the business I suppose? I had right smart trouble and been at a good deal of expense—" began Pokeberry doubtfully—"of course."

Dick was conscious of his master's approach to the cart. He gave a little convulsive twitch of his arms.

The next instant the Heavens opened.

"It seems to me you have him tied very tight," began the Major. Then his voice suddenly changed. "Why, man, d——n your soul! get in that cart and undo those ropes instantly. Why, you have nearly cut that boy's hands off. Instantly, don't you hear me?"

Tears again began to flow from under Dick's closed lids; but they were checked for a moment by his captor's surly protest.

"You better look out. He 's right dangerous —I had a heap of trouble gittin' him."

"Dangerous! The D——l!" cried the Major. "I'd like to know how you ever captured him if he was more dangerous than one of my sheep."

The snarl that Pokeberry gave was a solace to the negro in the cart; for it was one of the pet theories on the plantation that Pokeberry was a pig and sheep-stealer.

The Major's temper, however, now admitted of no delay. His voice had risen till it had in it the crack of a whip, and as he poured his wrath out on the negro-hunter his sarcasm stung like a lash. He declared that he would rather never have recovered his negro than have had one of his servants treated like a brute by a brute of a butcher.

The captor scowlingly loosed Dick from his bands, making a final plea for his reward. To which the Major scornfully assented, declaring, however, that he had learned a lesson and would never again offer a reward if his whole plantation ran away.

The transformation in the negro was remarkable. No sooner was he released than he struggled to his feet and grasping the Major's hand shook it violently, declaring with every asseveration that he was the best master in the world and that he would never again run away, not if every other man in the world tempted him.

The Major shook him off, giving him over his broad shoulders a half amused cut with his riding whip and ordering him to go to the house. "Or wait," he called, as he rode away, "perhaps you had better keep out of the way till I return," to which the negro with a low bow responded,

"Yes, suh; thankee masteh, I 'se gwine to do dat very thing," and with a muttered vow of revenge against Pokeberry he ran off. "I 'se gwine to git even wid you if I has to live a hunderd years," he muttered.

An hour later, when Major Landon rode up to his door, Dick, in a clean shirt, stood at his horse's head as though he had risen from the ground.

VII

THE eight years spent by Bruce Landon at school and college had, for Bruce, borne fruit in many ways. In none, however, more than in the change in the relationship between himself and his father. As soon as they were separated, and the friction of wills was wanting, they became great friends and mutual admirers. Bruce could not but admire the stern character of the old gentleman, who was inflexible in purpose, indomitable in will, and transparently honest in every word and act, however intolerant he might be and constitutionally incapable of yielding his opinion once formed on any subject. On the other hand, the high character of the boy, and the brilliant stand he had taken from the first, which he maintained until he graduated with distinguished honors, had caused his father very early in his course to forgive his boyish waywardness, and almost to overlook the infractions of collegiate discipline which were reported to him from time to time with more or less frequency. It was only when

Bruce was at home for the holidays, and the two were thrown together, that their wills came in conflict. It was soon apparent to both that the safest way to preserve the delightful relations between them was to remain separated. Thus it was, that Bruce was at home very little during the eight years of his school and college life, and usually spent his vacations in travel. When, therefore, he finally came home, he was almost a stranger.

As the carriage rolled up to the front door, and Bruce sprang out on the sanded walk, his father and mother both came running out to meet him, and both folded him in their arms, while the servants formed a half ring in the back-ground with their shining teeth and pleasant faces wishing him a hearty welcome. It was the only time Major Landon ever so far unbent.

The straight boy had become a tall, straight man, muscular and clean as a race-horse.

As, after the custom of the Landons, on the day he was twenty-one he stood for measurement on the threshold of the wide, wainscoted, picture-hung hall, with his back to the old massive mahogany front-door, where the Landons for generations, on attaining their majority, had been measured for height and breadth, there had hardly been one in all the list who had equalled him.

"Why, Bruce, you are the champion of three generations!" exclaimed his mother, looking up at his mark with pride.

"No; there have been several as tall; and one, the old general, my grandfather, was taller and broader," corrected his father, examining the door closely for the almost obliterated marks. The young man cast his eyes across the hall at the painting of his ancestor dressed in the military dress of Marlborough's time.

"He was a pretty good-looking fellow," he said, with lazy admiration.

"So is his descendant," smiled his mother.

"We got our height and our tempers both from him, did n't we?"

"No, sir; we may have got our stature from him, but we got our tempers from the devil," replied the Major. "No one but the devil can ever be held responsible for such devilish tempers."

"I quite agree with you," said the young man, complacently.

"I am pleased to receive the intelligence," replied the old gentleman, with a twinkle. "I believe it is the first time my views have ever received such a compliment.''

"Oh, no! we both agree in admiration of this lady, sir,'' said Bruce, putting his arm around his mother. Mrs. Landon smiled up at him, and the Major looked pleased at the delicate turn.

"There 's where you get your beauty,'' said Mrs. Landon, pointing across the hall to a full-length portrait of a lady, quite young, in rich brocade, with the long waist and satin petticoat of two generations before. The clear-cut face, with its dark eyes, was, indeed, beautiful, and would have been perfect, but for the haughtiness which shone even through the painter's art.

"I know where I got my beauty,'' said Bruce, leaning down and kissing his mother. Mrs. Landon blushed like a girl.

"But my grandmother was a beauty, was n't she?''

He went over and examined the portrait critically.

"It 's good enough for a Kneller,'' he said. "And that patrician face and old costume make her look like a young countess. One might fancy her turning her back on the prince himself.''

"She would have done it," said his father. "She turned her back on the President. He had not stood up to your grandfather. It lost my father the senatorship. But he always said it was cheap for the price."

Bruce found himself in a new life, almost wholly unknown to him. He had suddenly become the companion of the man who had always been to him the incarnation of pride and reserve. His father seemed not able to let him get out of his sight. If he went only to the stables, he invited him to come with him. He told him of all his affairs; talked over the politics of the county with him; consulted him; deferred to him. At the same time, he was treated like a distinguished guest. It was very new and very pleasant to him. The best wine was brought from the cellar: Madeira imported by his grandfather. The Major insisted on his riding his saddle-horse, and he himself rode another. No compliment could have been more marked and Bruce knew it. At last the wide gap between them had been bridged and father and son found mutual delight in each other's presence; for in the new relation each avoided the subject where there might be a chance of difference.

76

ON NEWFOUND RIVER

These years had wrought little appreciable change in the old neighborhood that included the two sides of Newfound. For there the world moved slowly and without much more evidence of change than the sluggish current of the mill-pond which one had to watch carefully to observe any perceptible movement in it. Even the lines in Major Landon's face had scarcely deepened and certainly Mrs. Landon's placid brow was as unclouded as it was when Bruce went off to school.

Perhaps, the chief change was simply the marked increase in the suspicions held of the singular tenant of the old Landon Hill place. Even this, however, was a natural growth. It had only deepened as the gullies had deepened with the washing of the ever recurrent rains, or as the pines had grown enfolding the old place with its occupants in an ever deeper seclusion.

This feeling had undoubtedly been fostered by certain occurrences which had taken place in this period. The new revival of the question of the Abolition of Slavery; the active propaganda carried on outside of the slave-holding section, under an instinct of philanthropy, no doubt, but one little appreciated

where it took away property, to set at naught
the fugitive slave laws; and the occasional
penetration of the agents of the Abolitionists
into the heart of the States, with the rumors
which ever followed thereon, served to keep
suspicion alive where there was the least apparent ground for it.

Certain of these agents of the Abolitionists
had been apprehended in a neighboring county
and public feeling was at a high tension. All
meetings by the negroes were discountenanced.
The appearance of every stranger was jealously
observed and he was expected to give an account of himself.

This feeling about the mysterious occupant
of the old Landon place on the other side of
Newfound had been largely augmented by the
efforts of Pokeberry Green. Pokeberry remembered a certain transaction of his not many
years back in which he had had a narrow escape
while pursuing his hazardous calling. He had
just succeeded in landing a too confiding negro
in the hands of a negro-trader in the far South
when a certain Dr. Browne had come along and
had recognized the man as the slave of some
friend of his and it had come near putting an
end, at least temporarily, to Pokeberry's trade.

Sometimes he shivered at the close graze he had had. He recalled the tall old man coming in just as he had gone for his money and the torrent of wrath he had poured out on the negro trader. He had just time to escape before the police came and even so he had lost the fruit of his toil. Fortunately, he had gone under a different alias from that by which he was known on Newfound. But he had met the old man for a moment face to face and had looked into his eyes. He knew now that it was Dr. Browne, the recluse of Landon Hill. He had taken the trouble to watch for him and this was the man. He was afraid that if they ever met again he himself would be recognized. Clearly it would not do to let the old man see him. If any one had to leave the county he preferred that it should be Dr. Browne. The only thing that stood in the way of this solution was that it would gratify Major Landon.

A DAY or two after his arrival Bruce was lounging in an easy-chair in the hall, looking over some fishing-tackle which he had exhumed. His mother was near-by engaged in some little household occupation; but with her smiling eyes mainly directed towards her son. Her real occupation was enjoying the sunlight of her boy's presence. The Major came in fuming. His neighbor's cows were in his corn.

"In there again!" he said to his wife as he laid his gloves and whip carefully on a table to one side. "I believe he thinks my cornfield belongs to him. I have stood it too long already. His cows have been living on me for twenty years, and now I am tired of it." He addressed Bruce, to whom it seemed like an echo from the past.

"My dear, I would not be hasty," said Mrs. Landon, soothingly.

"Hasty! you don't call it 'hasty,' when I have been fattening his cattle for twenty years, do you? He takes advantage of my patience. They graze in my cornfield as if it were nothing but his marsh-pasture, sir. But, at least, I 've got them for a while. I 've made Bailiff have them driven up into my barnyard, and there they shall stay till he sends for them."

He was speaking to Bruce and he did not mention that he had been particular to give orders that they should be well fed.

The reference to the pasture or the marsh, or something, brought up to Bruce the memory of a summer evening long since; of cow-bells tinkling faintly, and of drowsy sounds broken by a child's voice. How long ago it all appeared!

"What ever became of your queer old neighbor across the river, whose fish I used to catch, in defiance of the Decalogue?" he asked, looking up. "Is he dead?"

"Dead? No; that sort don't die. That is he, now," said his father. "It is a pity I did not let you catch his fish; I 've have got at least that much compensation, for he has been pasturing his old cows on my corn ever since. He drives them over, sir, regularly."

"Oh! now, my dear, you know he does n't do that," urged Mrs. Landon.

"Then they fly," said the Major, dryly.

"What a stir there used to be about it!" said Bruce, deep in reflection. "I remember there used to be a lot of talk about his being an Abolitionist, or in some way connected with those cattle. I suppose that has died out?"

"No, nothing of the kind. At least two negroes have disappeared from plantations about here in the last three or four years and I have grown suspicious that that old fellow is at the bottom of it. In fact, I feel certain of it."

"Oh! Now, my dear," put in Mrs. Landon,

"you do not feel certain. I would not suspect a man of such a vile crime without further proof."

"I feel as certain as I can without actual proof. That fellow Green—"

"I heard you say that you would not believe anything that creature said on oath."

The Major gave an exclamation.

"That 's what a man gets for ever making an admission to his wife. It is always brought up against him at the wrong moment."

"But, did you not say so?"

"Of course, I said so, and I would not; but —look at his own action. Why, he is as secret as a ferret. He has been there for twenty years and I have never had a glimpse of his face once."

"That is extraordinary," said Bruce, "I cannot understand it. That a man should withdraw himself from all intercourse with his kind is certainly most singular."

"Yes, and make it up by insisting that his neighbors shall have constant intercourse with his kine! That is what I object to."

Bruce laughed.

"I wonder you stand it, sir," he added, coming to the present issue. "I 'd break it up. I 'd sue him. I 'd do it at once."

"I 'm going to break it up. I 'll take your advice. I will give orders to my overseer to have a warrant served at once," said his father. "You are right. It will be tried next Saturday, at Jones's Crossroads. You 'd better go up; I 'll give you the case. You can flesh your maiden sword. I 'd like to have you there."

"No, I don't know that I will take the case," said the young man, languidly; "but I may. I 'll go up and see the fun, anyhow. I should have supposed that old man was dead. He appeared very feeble the only time that I ever saw him. There was something very mysterious about him."

"No, sir. Dead? Not he. He has compromised with the devil to live here always, and do his work for him, I believe. I have always believed he was in some way implicated in the disappearance of the negroes that have gone off from this neighborhood."

"What an old wretch he must be!" said Bruce, sympathetically. "What ever became of his little granddaughter, whose head was so full of nonsense? Has she ever married?"

"No; my neighbor, Sam Mills, tells me that she is there still. I have never seen her. She is cracked, too; has a school or something for the children on the other side, as though it were any of her business whether they are taught or not. Sam Mills says she has a great reputation, or would have, except that she keeps herself shut up at home all the time. An excellent man, Mills,'' he explained to his son. ''I have a very high esteem of him. An honest, upright man. The fact is, sir, there never was a braver, better people than our population, around through this country. That fellow has all the instincts of a gentleman. He is a philosopher. A remarkable man, sir. We agree on every subject. Now, if we had him as magistrate!—''

''She was a beautiful child. By Jove! sir, I believe I owe her my education,'' laughed Bruce, ignoring the tribute to his neighbor, Mills. ''I remember I swore to marry her, or something, and you shipped me off next day, post haste.''

''I have never seen her; but she is very unpopular in the neighborhood; at least, so Mills tells me. She is trying to missionaryize them.''

''I fancy they need it badly enough,'' said Bruce.

''Not at all, and if they do it is none of her business; they are quite satisfied. They have naturally resented her airs. It seems that she

thinks herself better than these other common
people around and will have nothing to do with
them.''

"Well—,'' said Bruce reflectively, ''they are
not common people—that is my recollection.—
I remember that the old fellow looked like—a
gentleman,'' he added, with a sudden recalling
of how much he had reminded him of his father.

The Major gave a sniff.

"I know nothing about his looks. I only
know they give themselves a great many airs
and our people resent it.''

"Oh, it is simply prejudice,'' said Mrs. Landon. ''The old man is very infirm, and she
stays at home to take care of him—that 's all.
People are so uncharitable.''

"Why, she has not had to stay at home for
six or eight years on that account, I reckon; and
I am not so well satisfied about his being infirm.
I am sure as to his moral infirmity; but his
bodily health is good enough, and too good for
his neighbors' security. If he had been a gentleman, he 'd have let me have that old place
back. I offered to let him name his own price.
Why, I called on him once, sir, and he never
even—''

"My dear,'' interrupted Mrs. Landon, **to**

whom the tale had long lost the charm of novelty, "I thought you had forgiven him."

"Forgiven him! No! I don't believe any one forgives unless he forgets," sniffed the Major.

"I would not be so unchristian," said his wife, whose face wore an expression of benediction. "Any one might suppose, my dear, from hearing you talk that you did nothing but cherish malice against that old fellow, yet you are always defending him against others and when he was ill not long ago, you were as miserable about it as though he were a member of the family."

"That is the weakness of my character," said her husband, "and even if my worst enemy is sick, I would not wish him to die like a dog, without having a doctor to kill him conventionally."

"Do they still keep themselves mewed up in their fortress as they used to do?" inquired Bruce, examining a line critically.

"Yes, sir; he has never been off the place since he came there, that I know of, except at night, and his daughter, or grand-daughter— whichever she is—confines herself in the same way. They stay at home and send the cows around."

"Well, it 's nobody's business except their own," suggested Mrs. Landon.

"Nobody's business!" exclaimed the Major, hotly, incontinently abandoning the position he had taken the moment before. "Yes, it is,—it 's everybody's business when a man behaves in that extraordinary way; it 's against the peace and dignity of the commonwealth! If it was n't for that lying rascal Pokeberry's saying so, I 'd believe that the reports about him are true, and that he is one of these Yankee Abolitionists."

"Why, my dear, they say he is just as kind and charitable as possible. When old Mrs. Mills was sick, he used to go over there every night and attend her, and he sent her medicine; and when Mr. Hackett had his house burnt—"

"That may all be a part of his scheme. It is a cheap price to pay for security. He ought to have been investigated and run out long ago," asserted the major.

"I thought she 'd have married before this," said Bruce, irrelevantly. "I wonder if his grand-daughter is pretty?" he added, addressing the question generally.

"They say she is quite a beauty," said his mother.

"A beauty! No. She is I believe rather good-looking, but I never heard she had beauty," sniffed the Major. "They say that Pokeberry Green is courting her."

"That creature! Why, he used to be a perfect young ruffian!"

"He is now," said his father; "a ruffian, a drunkard, and a thief. But he is after her, I understand,—at least, there 's some story about them."

"Oh, pshaw!" said Mrs. Landon. "I did hear that; but it was contradicted. I heard that he fancied himself in love with her, and had even ventured to speak to her once on the road; but she was so indignant that he slunk away. I think some one came up."

"That 's the reason she was indignant, I reckon," said the Major, dryly.

Mrs. Landon, with a woman's instinct to defend her sex, repudiated the idea warmly.

Bruce was so astonished at the idea of Pokeberry Green being the victim of the tender passion, that he led the conversation off to him, and the Major was soon engaged in telling what a turbulent element in the neighborhood he had become.

"He is the greatest scoundrel unhung," he declared in conclusion. "I am confident that he is a professional thief, and that he fools negroes into running away in order to get the reward for them by catching them. That runaway rascal of mine says he offered to take him to Philadelphia, and I believe him. Some day he will be hung. If we had a magistrate worth a button, we 'd have been rid of him long ago. But what can you do with such a fool as old Johnson? Bray him in a mortar, and he 'd still be a fool."

VIII

THE Major informed Bruce a few days later that he had acted on his advice and instituted the suit.

He told Mrs. Landon in the strict confidence of their chamber that Bruce was the wisest young man he ever knew.

"He reminds me very much of you," he said naïvely. Mrs. Landon repaid the compliment by declaring with equal sincerity that he was very much like him.

Bruce, however, was suddenly conscious of a feeling of regret that his father should have been so hasty. He had had no idea of being taken so literally. He determined that he would dissuade him from prosecuting his proceeding. When, however, he undertook this task he found it much more difficult than he had imagined. Having taken the step which he had contemplated so long, sufficient energy had been set in motion to require much more force to stop it than Bruce could bring to bear.

An afternoon or two after this, Bruce, wearied with talking over and advising about the pending warrant which his father had instituted against his neighbor for the damage inflicted by his cows, had taken a fishing-rod and sauntered down to the river. He tried several well-remembered holes, but the fish would not bite, and at length he found himself wandering in a rather listless way up the bank under the trees, uncertain whether to return home or not. Just where a path went down to the water's edge he discovered a boat tied to a small gum-tree which hung over the bank, and he determined to try the fishing on the other side.

As he paddled across the pond he experienced something of the exhilaration of boyhood. He let the skiff drift, dipped his hand down in the clear water and let it ripple against his wrist, thinking of the old days when he had so often done the same thing. The soft summer air just touched his cheek and brought the odors of the woods to him across the water like a faint memory of a land he had once known.

On the other side he tied his boat and climbed the bank to hunt for the old fishing-hole where he had caught the fish that afternoon so many years ago. When he had reached the spot he found that a tree had fallen over the bank, and its branches lay in the water, destroying all chance of sport at that place. So he retraced his steps and started up the pond through the woods. As he proceeded he fell into the path which led around the alder thickets by the old spring at the foot of the poplar, and a sudden thirst struck him to drink from the cool depths which bubbled from under the great flat rock. He followed the track, and reaching the spring, flung his rod on the ground. A gourd brown with age and use lay on the rock; but under an impulse guided by reminiscence he knelt down, and bending over, drank from the spring itself. He remained in that attitude for some minutes, looking into the clear, dark depths. He was drinking at the spring of memory.

How long ago it all was!

When he rose, he did not leave the spot; but sauntering to the great poplar, he flung himself at its foot and gave himself up to reverie. The sky overhead was blue and fleeced with long white films of cloud, which appeared quite stationary, and the dark green poplar boughs above him were unstirred by any breeze. The faint melody of a distant cow-bell in the marsh below him brought back his boyhood and filled him with drowsy content.

He was aroused by hearing a light step behind him, and he turned his head and looked around just as the "calush" of a bucket dipped into the water reached him.

A slender young woman, dressed in a plain light calico dress, spotlessly clean, was stooping over the spring, holding her skirts back with one hand, whilst with the other she lifted the dripping bucket. Bruce could not see her face; but he knew she was young from the pliant, supple figure, which the dress fitted closely, the easy pose, the plump arm, and the strong grasp of her hand on the bucket as she lifted it. A large, coarse straw hat was on her head; but its plainness was relieved by a loose twist of some white lawny stuff around it, tied on one side in a great bow-knot. She lifted the bucket, and set it on the rock. As she did so, her hair, suddenly loosened, slipped, and fell down on her shoulders in a rich crinkling mass. She removed her hat, and began to coil her hair. The curves and lines of her figure were clearly marked, from the small, well-poised head, round neck, and fine shoulders to the delicate ankle. She was as straight as an arrow. Bruce thought instinctively of a Diana he had once seen, straight and yet supple as a willow wand, with her slim form poised on her shapely feet and her face earnest with the ardor of the chase. He rose to his feet and leaned against the poplar. The slight noise he made caught her ear, and she turned quickly, raising her head. At the sight of a stranger so close to her, the rich color fled from her cheeks, leaving them a sudden white, and the large, dark eyes widened with startled surprise. Bruce recognized immediately the oval face, framed in loose masses of dim gold; but he saw that she did not know him.

Instinctively he took off his hat, and advanced with a smile, thinking, "By Jove! how pretty she is!"

"How do you do?" he said.

She drew herself up for a second, at being approached by a stranger. Then a look, at first of bewilderment, and presently of pleased recognition, came over her face. It was, however, not unmixed with embarrassment; for she blushed, and made a hasty little upward movement of her hand, as if to arrange her collar.

"Don't you know me?" he said, his eyes on her face.

"Yes." Her eyes were as level as his.

"I have come back."

He had the old engagement in his mind. He meant the speech to put them on the old friendly footing, for he felt that it was a kindness to her; and, perhaps, both his look and voice showed it.

"You are several years behind your time," she said calmly.

"Yes, I am; but it was not my fault; they sent me off to school."

He felt, as soon as he had given an excuse, that he had made a mistake, and had lowered himself in her eyes.

She bowed with so slight an inclination that he almost hoped she had not heard him.

"You have been at school some time?"

It may have been the faintest suggestion of sarcasm in her tone; it may have been the slight curve in her red lip; or it may have been Bruce's fancy; but he felt himself flush.

"I have never been home for any length of time," he said.

She looked at him calmly and her eyes seemed to pierce him.

"At least, in the fishing season, I mean; and this is the first time since that afternoon when you were a little girl, and came—hunting for your prince." He added the last clause tentatively.

"I have grown wiser since then," she said quietly.

"A sadder and a wiser woman?" he suggested with a smile.

"No, not sadder, only wiser. Only men are sad at gaining wisdom. It brings women peace."

"Have you never found the prince?"

"I have never sought for him. He does not exist."

Bruce felt somehow a vague regret. He had hoped she would think of him as she used to do; though he also hoped she did not divine his thoughts. He wondered at his embarrassment. He was accustomed to women, especially young women; and he was accustomed to have them appreciate any attention he might pay them. He felt that this girl, in her plain dress and her coarse straw hat, was inferior to the women he was accustomed to, and to himself. It was, therefore, a strange sensation to find himself wondering what she thought of him, and hoping that the result was in his favor.

"Do you know you are very pretty?" he said suddenly, breaking the ice, and throwing a look of admiration into his eyes, as he moved a step nearer to her. He intended to catch hold of her hand, and, perhaps, on the least encouragement, to kiss her. He had often tried the same tactics with eminent success. He held that every woman would be pleased to accept the incense.

She drew herself up slightly, but sufficiently to stop him.

"Do you know it is a liberty to take to say that to a woman unless you know her well?"

Her eyes looking straight into his flashed, and her lips were compressed with sudden resentment.

Bruce was taken quite aback.

"Confound it!" he thought; "I wonder if she really resents it. She cannot. It is not human."

"It is not usually considered a deadly insult," he said, with an attempt at a smile, trying to cover his retreat, but feeling very silly.

"I suppose not to the women to whom you are accustomed to saying it." The tone was icy.

It put him on the defensive.

"No; I don't have the provocation often. I am accustomed to saying what I please, and to doing what I please," he added audaciously, after a second's pause, looking her full in the eyes.

The girl drew herself up, and gave him a look of defiance, which subsided into what appeared much like contempt.

"I have to go," she said quietly, leaning over and taking up her hat.

"May n't I go with you?" asked Bruce, willing to make amends. "Let me carry your bucket."

"No, thank you. Good evening."

She leaned over and picked up her bucket, and without deigning another glance walked slowly up the hill, her pliant figure swaying a little to one side under the weight of the bucket.

Bruce, leaning against the poplar, watched her until she was out of sight, and then going to his boat, crossed the pond, and went home. As he walked up the path he had a perplexed, absent air, as of a man who had sustained a loss, but who could not tell just what. Who would have thought to find Diana at that spring! As for "Diana" herself, it is certain that she positively hated him as she bore her bucket up the path and had she had a quiver on her straight back, would have shot several of her sharpest arrows at that tall young fellow

98

with his cool gray eyes and self-assured way. She would show him. But as she thought it, her heart relented. It came back again and again, however, and she sharpened her arrows every time she thought of him.

Bruce made up his mind that he would induce his father to dismiss his warrant if it were possible. It would serve to help him recover the ground which he felt he had lost with Dr. Browne's granddaughter. He found, however, that he had a difficult task before him. The Major like many another man had reached the position where he confounded his personal feeling with a public duty.

Moved by the desire to withdraw his thoughts from so dangerous a quarter, his father and mother made an effort to interest him in the social life of the neighborhood. All the gentry within reach were invited to come and "spend the day," and sundry pretty girls among them fluttered in their white dresses in the summer evenings among the shrubbery of Landon Hall. But it was plain to Mrs. Landon and she made it plain to the Major, that Bruce, however much he laughed and rode and sang with them, remained untouched by the sparkle of their eyes or the cadences of their soft voices.

Then Major Landon, having failed in one direction, tried another and a new bait. It had always been his ambition to have his house once more represented in public life. The Landons with their prestige and intellect were well fitted to shine in public life, and in the past had held high official station, representing, as was natural to them the aristocratic and federal side of political questions. But the balance had shifted a generation before, and as we have seen from the Major's hint to Bruce on his return home, a breach had come between Colonel Charles Landon and the head of his party, and Bruce's grandmother had publicly cut the President to the final destruction of her husband's political hopes, but to his vast personal gratification. The chance of success had been too small since then for the Major ever to enter politics; even had he not settled down to a state of content too profound to break with the exactions of a political canvass where he must conceal his decided views or at least modify them to meet the views of a constituency strongly democratic. Now, however, that his son was grown up and gave promise of adaptability and popularity auspicious of future success, the Major's dormant ambition awoke. He had long hoped that Bruce would restore the lost political prestige of the family and had, indeed, been quietly preparing for this coveted end. He had begun to cultivate certain of his neighbors who differed from him; he had made overtures to men who bored him. He had even repressed his tendency to characterize those who disagreed with him with his caustic speech which burnt like an acid.

The time had now come, he felt, when Bruce should at least begin to prepare for the career which he had marked out for him. He believed that it was only his want of occupation which had made him of late distrait and indifferent to his surroundings. A suggestion from Mrs. Landon that Bruce had an ambition to write he scouted with disdain. "Write poetry! Tell him to read Dryden and Pope. These modern poets either give milk and water slops like Tupper, or rank infidelity and wickedness like Byron. I 'd rather have Landon Hall kept up than be the father of Milton."

He had no doubt that this suggestion would bring Bruce to his senses even if Mrs. Landon had not with her maternal partiality rather overstated Bruce's tendencies and desires.

Accordingly he broached to Bruce one day the subject of politics. It might be as well at the outset to give him an insight into a few

101

plain principles. To his astonishment Bruce announced that he had always thought of entering politics, but on the Democratic side. The Major simply gasped and for a moment sat in silence overwhelmed by what was very near to emotion. A Democrat! The idea was so preposterous, so tragic, that his mind staggered. His wrath did not even awaken, or at least was held in check.

Bruce, feeling his emotion, said with a certain sympathy and with real affection, "That is the reason I have not offered to take any active part in politics, sir. I have not wished to do what I knew would give you any pain." The Major's reply was little more than a grunt, though it was doubtless intended for a polite acceptance of his son's apology. The latter proceeded, "I believe that, as the Constitution says, all men were created free and equal."

"The devil you do!" snapped the Major. "In the first place the Constitution contains no such nonsense. I presume that you refer to Thomas Jefferson's high sounding pronunciamento in the Declaration of Independence; but if you believe that, then you believe a bigger lie than even Thomas Jefferson was silly enough to commit himself to. For, at least, he knew from his property-lists that all were not born as free and as socialistic as he was in his utterances, he never meant to say they were all created equal.''

Bruce, in some confusion, corrected his mistake. He meant, of course, to say, he explained, ''created equal'' and he could not hold with a party that created class-distinctions. This was too much for his father.

''I 'd like to know where you 'd be, sir, if it were not for your derided class-distinctions. In the name of Heaven! Has a gentleman no rights which the rabble need respect?''

''The same rights with all others under the law.''

''And pray, sir, who made the laws? Who wrung them from a despotic tyrant and transmitted them to us as our heritage?''

''Well, I suppose our fathers did,'' admitted Bruce, whose ideas of history were rather hazy.

The Major pressed his advantage.

''I suppose, as you think that all men are born free, you think slavery a sin?''

''I do.''

The answer steadied the older gentleman.

''Bruce, don't be a fool,'' he said slowly. ''Don't you go and fling away your bread and butter.''

He rose and stalked from the room.

IX

BRUCE took to fishing industriously after this; and whether it was that the fish would not bite on his own side of the pond, or whatever the cause, he availed himself fully of the permission given so long ago by the old doctor, and every afternoon found him lounging, rod in hand, up the bank, or as frequently lying on the ground by the spring on the doctor's side of the water.

It was remarkable how often he became thirsty, and how long a distance he would walk to drink at the spring that bubbled from under the rock. Sometimes he spent the whole afternoon lounging in the shade of the great poplar. He, however, was not fortunate enough to see Miss Reid again.

Failing to meet her who now had begun to be much in his thoughts, he fell to a resource which had stood in stead even that ardent youth who haunted the forests of Arden. In other words, he indited a sonnet to his hard-hearted and shy young nymph and stuck it as though casually on a twig that grew beside the poplar spring.

ON NEWFOUND RIVER

It cost him much labor, but some of the labor had already been expended in previous attempts to celebrate other girls during his college days.

It ran thus:

TO DIANA AT THE SPRING

In æons old when life was young and sweet,
Diana, weary of the eager chase,
Was wont to seek full oft some trysting-place
Well loved of all her train—some cool retreat
Of crystal founts, deep-verdured from the heat
Of sultry noon, wherein each subtle grace
Of snowy form and radiant flower face,
Narcissus-like, Goddess and nymph might greet.

Diana long hath fleeted o'er the Main,
The founts which erst she loved are all bereft;
No more on violet banks her feet are set,
Silent her silvern bugle, fled her train;
One spot alone of all she loved is left;
This poplar-bowered spring is Goddess-haunted yet.

This effusion did not altogether satisfy him, for his taste was fastidious and not wholly uncultivated; but he took much pains to hang the paper on a bush so that it might appear to have caught there carelessly. He felt tolerably sure that Miss Diana would see it, and would not go far wrong in her guess as to its authorship.

After this he continued to fish sedulously;

but for several days his sonnet hung on the twig and his heart sank. Had he but known it, however, though the paper remained untouched on the twig, Miss Diana had seen it and, in fact, had copied it on the sly, after looking carefully about to see that no one was observing her. Nor had she much doubt as to who the young Orlando was. And though her very well chiseled nose took the least upward turn, it is possible that she thought more of young Orlando than she had thought of Bruce Landon for several days.

Thus, her thoughts were a court in which a gray-eyed offender was continually, every few hours, arraigned, duly convicted and sentenced, and then as regularly recommended to mercy and pardoned.

At last Bruce reached the point where he felt that he must see the girl he had offended.

One afternoon he had been up to the spring as usual, and had spent some time there enjoying the quiet which was broken only by the crackling of leaves, the occasional note of a bird, and the sound of two cow-bells far up the pond. The bells mellowed by the distance had grown fainter and fainter, and had finally ceased. He had sauntered up the stream in the opposite direction to that he usually took. He had with some difficulty crossed a small creek which ran into the pond, and was making his way along a little path, through the thick growth of pines, gums, alders, and other bushes, when he was almost startled to meet in the narrow cowtrack an old negro woman. She was tall and thin, and exceedingly black; and her short gray hair peeped out from under the pointed white handkerchief bound around the top of her head.

Bruce recognized instantly the old woman with whom he had had the interview years ago on the occasion when he had carried the fish back to Dr. Browne. She had evidently been walking rapidly, for her face was streaming with perspiration. She was startled at meeting a stranger there in the woods; but Bruce greeted her kindly, which seemed to set her at her ease. "Yo' sarvent, marster," she said, stepping out of the path, and courtesying with a quaint little bend at the knees.

Bruce spoke to her kindly.

"You ain' see nuthin' o' no cows down dat away, is you, marster?" she asked doubtfully.

"No, I have not," said Bruce. "I heard the cow-bells over that way somewhere, a half-hour or more ago." He indicated the direction in

107

which he was going. "Have your cows bells on?"

"Yes, suh; bofe on 'em," she said. "I done been up dat away, an' ain' see nuthin' on 'em. I mightly feared dee done gone crost de pawn an' git in Mr. Landon's corn agin; but I ain' see whar dee cross nowhar, up dere." She stood still in evident perplexity.

"How do they get across?" asked Bruce.

"I 'clar,' marster, I don' know. They 's jes' natchel rovers; they git whar bud can't fly."

"Why do you let them run down here?" inquired Bruce. "Why do you not keep them up?"

"Well, to tell you de truf, marster," said the old woman, simply, "we ain' got nuthin' to feed 'em on. We 'bleeged to le' 'em run down heah. Dee 's all de 'pendence we got. You see, ole marster, he 's so ailin' now he cyarn git 'bout to do nuthin'; an' Polium—he 's my ole man,—he so cruppled up wid rheumatis, he cyarn hardly do nuthin', an' all he kin do is to wait on ole marster, an' help him de little bit he 's able to do, an' to fish. Sometimes he ketch some right smart." She said this almost pathetically. "An' de cows an' de chickens is we main d'pendence."

108

Bruce put his hand into his pocket and made a mental estimate of the amount of change he found there.

"We did n't use to have much trouble wid 'em," she went on, "so long as dee had plenty o' grass on dis side; but now dee done fine de way 'cross we have to watch 'em study all de time. We do right well as long as my young mistis or I one kin watch 'em; but ef we teck our eye off 'em now, dee gone."

Bruce was all attention now, and the old woman, with feminine instinct recognizing his sympathy, was glad to relieve her troubles by imparting them to another.

"Dee got 'way de other day when ole marster was so po'ly, and got into Mr. Landon's corn over yonder,—right over 'cross de pawn," she pointed, "an' he meck de overseer drive 'em up, an' put 'em in he lot. I had to go over dere after 'em. He overseer did n't warn' le' me have 'em at fust. Toonsey she went back right smart, an' Princess she gone back a heap, from not being milked reg'lar, you know?" she explained.

Bruce nodded.

"But I so glad to fine 'em an' git 'em back agin, I ain' mine nuthin'. At fust, I begin to think I ain' gwine git 'em no mo' de way dat man talk; but I promise him faithful I would n't le' 'em git in de corn no mo', an' den he le' me bring 'em long, an' he suin' ole marster 'bout de corn. De man come heah one day las' week an' gi' him de paper.''

She turned, preparatory to continuing her search.

''Wait a minute,'' said Bruce. He paused irresolutely. ''How do you live?'' he asked abruptly.

''Well, we got some chickens, an' we sell de aigs an' de butter,'' she explained, ''an' sometimes we ketch some fish.''

''Here, let me give you something,'' said Bruce. He raked up all the change in his pocket, and handed it to her, half shamefacedly.

Her thanks were mute astonishment. She looked first at him, and then at her hand, full of the silver he had given her, and which she held out half-way to him, as if not certain that he had not made a mistake.

''Come on; I will help you find your cows,'' he said. ''You go that way, and I will go this,'' and he plunged ahead through the bushes.

He found in the search a new pleasure. It brought back the zest of his boyhood; and he went in and out along the edge of the pond, examining carefully every place where the cows could have gone down to the water. At last he came on their tracks, and following them, found that the cows had gone up around the pond, and had crossed over near its head, where the water was shallow. A less keen eye might have missed the trail. The difficulty of getting over was considerable; but the faint jangle of bells reached him from the other bank. The cows were evidently in the cornfield, on the opposite side.

As Bruce had pledged himself, there was no help for it; so, after going up a little higher, he was able to get across, though not without difficulty. The cows were found; and after an exciting chase through the corn, in which a great deal of grain was trampled down, Bruce got them to the point where they had crossed, and drove them back. He was walking carefully on the hummocks, thinking of his boyhood when he tried to imitate Dick Runaway, and was nearly over, when his foot slipped, and he went down into the water to his waist. He gave expression to an objurgation at the cows, and climbed out, dripping. Just then, looking up, right before him on the bank stood the young girl he had met before. A distressed expression was on her face and Bruce awoke to a sudden sense of her supreme charm.

"How do you do?" said Bruce, feeling that he must cut a sorry figure.

"Did they get into your corn again?" she asked. "I am so dreadfully sorry. We will keep them up hereafter."

"No, you will not," said Bruce, almost roughly.

She misinterpreted his reply. "Indeed, I will; it was an entire accident that they got away to-day. My grandfather was sick, and I just—"

"I don't care anything about that," said Bruce.

She misunderstood him; but he proceeded.

"I promised your old woman to find her cows for her, and as they set the fashion of wading, I had to follow it."

She said "Thank you" so cordially, and added, "I 'm so afraid that you will catch cold," so solicitously, that Bruce forgot his unpresentable appearance, and said:

"I don't mind it the least bit. When I was a boy I used to know every foot of the pond, and I have hunted often, wet to the skin, almost

112

for days at a time." He was after gaining
time. To find her so changed in her manner to
him had suddenly changed the world. To have
her leave him suddenly looked like putting out
the sun. To gain a respite he would promptly
have changed his tone, and have avowed himself
ready to die with cold. She started up the path,
and allowed him, without anything being said
about it, to walk with her down the pond under
the overhanging boughs of the willows, taking
the easy pace at which the two cows lazily
sauntered homewards along the narrow track,
one behind the other, stopping now and then to
browse on the grass or young bushes beside the
way.

Before the walk was over, they were on terms
of confidence. Bruce had forgotten the difference in their stations. She told him of her fond-
ness for the woods, and of how, as a girl, she
used to know every path in the pines, and every
nook on the pond.

"I used to like to fish," she said; "but I don't
love my frogs, and I cannot handle them as if
I did. I cannot bear to see the poor fish struggling and gasping for breath. Besides that,
there is a dreadful man who comes down here
sometimes and frightens me. He seems to

haunt the place," she explained. She had met him once or twice. He had once stopped her, and attempted to detain her in conversation. She described him: "He has a great purplish mark across his throat, and looks brutal and insolent. He always carries a gun."

Bruce had no difficulty in recognizing Poke-berry. As she lifted her eyes with the timid expression in them, born of the recollection of the interview, he was filled with a sudden desire to throttle the brute who dared to frighten her.

Nothing arouses a man's tenderness so surely as a woman's showing fear, and yet silently confiding in his protection.

I will see that you are not molested fur-ther," said Bruce, quietly. His heart was bounding at the thought of a chance to counter-balance the false step he had made when he induced his father to institute his suit.

"Oh, you must not do anything to him. Please don't," she said quickly, stopping and making an earnest little gesture of entreaty towards him. "He always carries a gun, and I 'm so afraid he would shoot you." She looked at him with anxious, uplifted, large eyes.

"I will take care that he does n't do that," said Bruce, his heart leaping with pleasure.

"I admire courage more than anything in the world," she said naïvely. "I suppose it is because I am so afraid of everything myself. I remember I used as a child to make myself perform things that I was afraid of, just to have the sense of overcoming my fear."

Bruce, with a look of admiration in his eyes, asked what sort of things she referred to.

"Why, I remember once making myself go to the old graveyard in the dark. I was dreadfully afraid of the dark. I was in a terrible fright. Ugh!" She gave a little shiver at the recollection. "The grape-vines hanging down from the old trees were in the dark all like snakes. They just crawled and made a noise. Of course it was only the leaves rustling, but I was such a coward I nearly fainted. It was so creepy. And occasionally I have had to go at night to carry things for my grandfather to people about here."

"What sort of things?" asked Bruce, remembering the stories he had heard.

"Medicines and food." Her simplicity made Bruce ashamed of his question.

Bruce had a look in his eyes which showed what he thought of such cowardice. He for the first time noted the firm lines about her mouth and chin. Somehow, they reminded him of his father. He said to her:

"Did you ever hear of Marshal Turenne saying of his knees, which were trembling as he mounted his horse to command in a great battle, that if they knew where he was going to take them that day they would shake more than they were shaking then?"

"Oh! it was not courage in me," she smiled; "it was nothing but pride. I was always proud enough; in fact, it is one of my deadly sins,— at least, so grandpapa always says. Mammy used to call it obstinacy. I remember once, as a child, actually starving myself as a practice, because Katherine was starved into submission by Petruchio. I wanted to be able, by practice, to meet my Petruchio when he should come."

Bruce's face was a study as he listened to this history.

"I fancy you would have no trouble on that score," he smiled.

"I don't know. Perhaps— Was n't it silly? I kept it up till I got really sick. Then grandpapa gave me some dreadful stuff to take. That cured me. No Petruchio ever came; but had he done so, he would not have conquered me by starvation. Grandpapa says I got it from him. But his pride is noble. I have seen him endure torture without a groan. You do not know how brave he is. He is almost blind, and will soon be quite so; yet he never says a word of it.''

There was a look of softness in her face as she spoke of her grandfather, which, following the expression of determination that it had borne just before, made her more beautiful than ever. Diana had changed for the young man to the softer and more bewitching Venus. Bruce Landon looked at her with new interest. He had never met any one just like this until now. He had never taken in her full beauty before. He was conscious that he had suddenly grown bashful. He hardly dared to touch her hand as he helped her over a fallen tree across the path. Her warm touch thrilled him as her hand lay in his. He had never noticed before what a delicate, shapely hand she had: the fingers long and tapering, the wrist so small, the skin so fine. He was overcome with a sudden sense of her beauty; her pliant figure, her white throat, the curves of her cheek and chin, the delicate, rich mouth, the white teeth, the fine nose, the changing color, the large,

117

lustrous, sweet eyes,—they entranced him, made his heart beat.

"You must go back now," she said gently, as they neared the top of the hill. "I have to make a cup of tea for my grandfather. I have no doubt he has been expecting me for a half-hour."

"Cannot I go with you?" Bruce found courage to ask. "I should like very much to meet him. I did once, as a boy."

"No; he never sees visitors," she said simply, with a little smile. "He is a great invalid. Good-by." She held out her hand.

He took it, and pressed it.

"Good-by."

X

MARGARET passed quite through the pines, and reached the opening beyond which was what was once the yard, but was now, except for a strip of flower-border and turf which showed care, simply a tangle of bushes and briars. Instead of going on to the house, she passed along the path to an outhouse on the side of the yard, and went in. A moment later she came out, and going over to a little wood-pile, began to pick up some chips.

It was perhaps a quarter of an hour afterwards that she left the old kitchen, and passed along to the house with a waiter covered with a napkin, on which were an old-fashioned teapot and cream jug, and a cup and saucer of old blue china.

As she entered the house, a high, querulous voice sounded from an inner room,

"Margaret! Margaret! Margaret!"

"Yes, grandpapa, I 'm coming," she called, quickening her step, and opening a door on the left of the long passage.

119

The room she entered was furnished as a bedroom. The few articles of furniture, though old and worn, were of handsomer workmanship than anything about the place would have prepared one to expect. A high and old massive, carved mahogany bedstead, with tall tester reaching up to the top of the low-pitched room, took up half of one side of the apartment; and the two or three straight-backed chairs and the legs of the round table were carved with an elaborateness which told of a former age.

By the open window, propped up with pillows, in an armchair, sat an old man, whose black, deep-set eyes, gleaming from beneath his shaggy white brows, gave the only suggestion of color in his pallid face. The thin, sharp face, the keen, aquiline nose, the stern pose of the white head, and the restless, deep eyes gave the invalid a resemblance to an old gray eagle, which was not diminished by the long, thin hands, which, as Margaret entered, clutched the arms of his chair nervously, as he faced the door.

"Well, where have you been?" he demanded in that querulous tone which affection sometimes employs, when it dwells in the breast of an invalid, as the girl entered the room. "Here

120

I have been shouting myself hoarse for two hours." His words were a complaint, but, as his eyes rested on the sweet vision before him, his tone lost the accent of chiding and became half humorous.

His granddaughter, before she answered, crossed the room, and placed the waiter on the small table. Then she approached the invalid, and proceeded deftly to arrange his pillows. There was a little flush on her face as she met the keen eyes.

"Where have I been?" she smiled, as she smoothed the creases and patted the white napkin. "Well, I have been rubbing my lamp, and demanding a spring that bubbles up hot tea, and I have been getting a pitcher of cream from the cow that jumped over the moon,—and all for the most spoilt baby that ever cried 'two hours' on a stretch,—and here they are."

She stooped over, and kissed the old man tenderly on the forehead. As she turned away to bring the table closer, the expression on the invalid's face changed, and the hawk eyes followed her with a new tenderness.

"Ah yes, you are a dear little fairy," he said, "and I am an old tyrant."

"Oh no! you are not; you shall not say such

things of yourself. You are my dear old grand-papa." She kissed him again.

"I am the worst enemy you ever had on earth," said the old man, bitterly.

"You are nothing of the kind, and you are not to talk that way. It always excites and fatigues you, and you must stop it. You know that you promised me never to speak that way. Here, your tea is getting cold. No; you must drink it at once."

She held the cup to him with a pretty authority, and the old man accepted it.

Bruce walked home like a man in a trance. He was divided between his recollection of Margaret Reid and his determination to persuade his father to dismiss his warrant. When, however, he reached the house, he found his father seated on the porch, in a state of high indignation. He was indulging in a philippic against his neighbor across the river.

"Why, sir," he said, taking Bruce into his audience in the middle of a sentence; "why, sir, he has turned his cows into my cornfield again! Right on the eve of the warrant! He's simply flouting me!"

Bruce declared that it was impossible.

"Impossible! I tell you that it is so. I

heard the cow-bells myself down there in my field; and when my overseer went down there, he found where they had been chasing around, trampling down my best corn. He saw the track of the man that was with them. I believe he comes over and cuts the corn regularly."

"Well, the man was driving them out," said Bruce.

"No such thing. Bailiff says he saw where he came up from the water."

"Well, I know he was," asserted Bruce; "for I drove them out myself."

"Ah, you were acting as cowherd for old Browne?—or perhaps it was his daughter?" said his father, with that dry, acrid tone which burned like a hot iron.

The young man winced. He set his teeth hard together.

"I hope that you will pasture them somewhere else hereafter except in my best corn," continued his father.

"I am not his cowherd," said Bruce; "but, perhaps, if you would keep up your fences, you would not have to lay the blame on your neighbors."

"You had better appear at the trial, and air your views there. They may be deemed of more

value by the magistrate than I consider them.
He is a fool. If he had n't been, I 'd have
brought the warrant years ago.''

It was the old gentleman's manner, not his
words, which cut.

Bruce remembered his own advice to him to
bring the warrant.

''I shall not go to the trial at all,'' he said.

''Ah! you will not? You will do me the favor
to remain neutral? Thank you.''

The Major's fine nose looked even thinner
than ever, and the nostrils dilated.

Bruce had never been so patient before. He
thought of the picture the old negro woman
had drawn of their poverty, and it brought him
self-control.

''They are very poor—'' he began, and
paused. ''If you knew how poor they are, you
would not be so hard on them,'' he broke out
suddenly.

The Major never intended to be hard on any
one; but he was thoroughly angry now, and was
blind to everything.

''You have been investigating the matter, and
sitting in judgment on me? You had better go
and ask Johnson to let you try the case. He
usually makes up his mind before he hears any

evidence, and you would be a very good associate for him. I don't know how poor your protégé is; but he ought to be rich, as he has been fattening his cattle in my corn so long."

He rose and marched into the house.

THE owner of Landon Hill was sitting on his verandah in the dusk, the last light of the evening sky falling softly on his white hair and beard. Seen in this dim light the strong lines of his careworn face, the high nose and deep-set, dark eyes which gave his countenance at times something of an eagle look, were softened until he might have been simply an old man dreaming of the past. And, in fact, many dreams were passing through his mind—of a past, full of sunshine and shadow; but where one shadow ever rested; of a present where the shadows were increasing; and of a future where there appeared but darkness for the one thing on earth that time had left for him to love. When he was gone who would there be to take care of Margaret, the one sunbeam in his somber life. He would not have her go back to the far South. Yet it might be the only thing left for her to do. Had he done right in sacrificing to his pride all her interest? Was it right in him not to claim his own where her future depended on it? Yet, if he claimed them what part would the desire for revenge have played? And when revenge was gratified what would he do with the negroes? He had long since made up his mind on this point.

Into this reverie broke the sound of a footstep coming across the grass.

A footstep may indicate a person's intention and frame of mind almost as clearly as the voice, and this was just such a step. Indeed, the visitor had for some time been watching outside the yard gate, waiting for the daylight to die down and to be sure that no one else was about; and even under cover of the dusk he came forward with a cringing sort of motion, a step as of a hunter or of a beast of prey, noiseless and crafty.

"Who is that?" asked the old man peering through the dusk.

"Good-evening, Dr. Browne."

"Good-evening. Who are you?" demanded the person addressed.

"My name 's Green. I guess you may have heard of me."

"I don't recall it. Excuse my not rising. I am suffering somewhat with an old wound which interferes with my locomotion. Won't you take a seat? What can I do for you?"

"Oh, not much. I just called to see if I could n't do something for you. I used to know some of your friends down South."

"You did? Whom, for instance?" There was a sudden coldness in the old man's voice and he turned his eyes upon his visitor with so keen a glance in them that that impervious person began to stammer. He, however, after a moment recovered himself.

"I used to know Mr. Le Drus."

"Well you knew no good of him," snapped the old Doctor. "The negro-trader! A greater rascal I never knew even in that nefarious profession. Not content with what he made out of his hellish traffic, he bought stolen negroes."

His visitor cleared his throat and shifted his seat uneasily. "I don't know anything about that. I never had any dealings with him; in fact, I was against him myself."

The old man, however, was too intent on the memories awakened by the name to pay much attention to the other's words.

"I found him with one of my father's negroes —I mean a negro I used to know," he corrected himself quickly,—"that I knew was stolen, and if it had not been for—if he had not given him up I 'd have had him arrested. He bought him from the man who stole him."

Pokeberry cleared his throat. "What did he say his name was?"

"I did not learn his name, but I should know him if I ever saw him again." Pokeberry slowly and stealthily pulled up his collar.— "Yes, I 'd know him—and he 'd know me." Again the younger man cleared his throat, and could he have been seen, it might have been noticed that his face had whitened and the perspiration stood on his brow.

"Where did he say he got him," he asked after a pause.

"He did not say. I could not get him to confess."

The other gave a sigh of relief, "Ah," and when he spoke next he had changed his tone.

"I 'm like you. I don't believe in slavery," he said insinuatingly. "I don't think one man 's got any right to hold another in bondage. The Lord did not intend it."

"You appear to be in the Lord's confidence," observed Dr. Browne dryly.

"Don't you believe it right to set 'em free?" asked the visitor.

"I set mine free; but I do not believe that I have a right to steal another man's property." Pokeberry appeared to be pondering. He moved so as to get himself in deeper shadow.

"Why don't you claim your rights?" he asked suddenly. Dr. Browne wheeled on him swiftly.

"What's that to you? What do you know about my rights?" he demanded. Pokeberry laughed uneasily.

"I know a good deal more than people think."

"Have you any business with me?" enquired the old gentleman. Pokeberry was pondering. He could not conceive of any man's lying perdue unless he had something to conceal which he would pay for keeping quiet.

"I know what your name is," he said as though he were merely finishing his last sentence.

"Is that all you have to say?"

"How much will you give me not to tell it?" demanded Pokeberry.

Dr. Browne raised himself from his chair and faced him, peering at him in the dusk.

"I know who you are now," he said slowly.

"You know the road you came here by. Take it and never put your foot here again. I don't know what object you had in coming; but by —! if I ever hear of you interfering with my business, old and broken as I am, I will hunt you down and hand you over to the authorities."

Pokeberry, bully as he was, was taken aback by the old man's fierceness.

"I did not come to threaten you. I did not come to speak out of the way. I come to do you a good turn."

"I want nothing from you. Go." The old fellow pointed imperiously through the dusk towards the gate and the younger man rose and slunk away. As he walked along he mumbled a curse. "He must be gotten rid of."

He would get even with him if it took him all his life. But it would clearly not do to let him see him again.

XI

THE warrant brought by the Major against the old "doctor" was the absorbing topic on Newfound. Other men had brought warrants. Indeed, Squire Johnson sat monthly on the fourth Saturday in every month, at Jones's Crossroads, and dispensed justice among the neighbors, at an average of one dollar a case. But the Major had never gone to law before. He had always boasted that he had never had a suit in his life. His neighbor's cows had been running on him for years, and he had contented himself with growling about it, or, when he was particularly exasperated, with threatening to sue for damages. He had never carried the threat into execution; some said, only because Squire Johnson was magistrate, whilst others ascribed it to a better motive.

At any rate, now, after long waiting, the Major, who had for twenty years scouted the justice, and ridiculed with his biting speeches the pitiful dissensions of his neighbors, had broken his boasted record and had gone to law himself.

"Yes; I am a fool, too," he admitted caustically to one of his friends who rallied him on his taking the step of an appeal to law after having so often inveighed against it. "Yes; I am a fool like the rest. But if I remain so different from my neighbors, they all impose on me and eat me up."

On the morning of the trial Bruce Landon and his father met at breakfast. The Major's face was unusually grim, and the look in his deep-set eyes, and the expression on his thin, clean-shaven lip, were not auspicious of peace. He was evidently girded up for battle. Bruce also was prepared for whatever might befall. His morning greeting, as he entered the long breakfast-room, was suspiciously polite; but his face was set with a look of defiance, and every movement was a declaration of resistance. The meal, however, passed off without an outbreak; indeed, almost in silence. Bruce was thinking of Margaret Reid, and the Major was thinking of his disappointment in his son. The Major, having finished, rose and marched out of the room, shutting the door behind him with a slam. He might have been heard walking backwards and forwards with a sharp, quick step from one room to another, as he made his preparations to set out, and when he left the house his tread was that of a grenadier. He carried in one hand a heavy riding-whip, and in the other an old law-book which he had been studying assiduously for several days, and which had the leaves turned down in many places. At the rack he gave the volume to a negro boy, and calling to another to tell Mr. Bailiff that he had gone, he mounted his horse and rode away.

Bruce spent the morning in lounging listlessly about the house. He tried reading, writing, and several other things; but his favorite authors palled on him, and his pen refused to finish the sentence he began. He saw nothing but Margaret Reid, heard nothing but her voice. He felt that he had been largely to blame in setting his father on to bring the warrant. At last, about midday, he took his fishing-tackle and strolled down towards the pond.

The little yard at Jones's Crossroads was quite full an hour before the time set for the hearing. The neighborhood had turned out, and the little store did a thriving business in calico, nails, striped candy and whiskey.

The first person to arrive connected with

the case was Hall, the constable. He was watched with great interest as he tied his horse to the fence, and took off with exaggerated deliberation his saddle-bags. They were known to contain his official papers, and were watched with expectation approaching to awe by the crowd in the little yard across the road. They insensibly lowered their voices, and gazed at the officer as if they expected some kind of animal to jump out of his leather pockets. He entered the little yard, greeting every one he met with that exaggerated cordiality and condescension which usually appertains to public office. A group immediately surrounded him, to whom he began to tell of his visit to Dr. Browne's.

"I was just about to pin the summons on the do' and come away," he said, "when roun' the house there came the pretties' young lady that my eyes ever see, or ever expec' to see." He took out a bundle of papers, and resting his finger on it, continued: "I have done made the return on thar that I explained the nature of the summons to her, and that she was over sixteen; but the fact is I did n't do much explainment, and the Lord knows I don't know whether she 's sixteen or not. I know I 'd ruther fling

up the orfis than 'a' axed her. But I jes' 'lowed
she could n' 'a' growed all that pretty in less
than sixteen years, that 's all. Don't you think
I am right, Sam?"

As Hall was a widower of some months'
standing, this reasoning struck his audience as
irresistible.

"Talk about Pokeberry? Why, she would n'
look at him 'cept to kick him out of her way,"
he said, as a stout, heavy man approached the
group. His face was a deeper red than that of
even the sunburned men about him. His eyes
were bloodshot, and his gait was slightly un-
steady. He caught the closing part of the constable's speech, and gave a harsh, grating
laugh, which he followed with a storm of oaths.
One of the little hounds at his heel was so un-
fortunate as to get in his way; he gave the
beast a savage kick which sent it off yelping
with pain.

"Pokeberry, you agree with me, I know?"
said the constable; at which sally there was a
general laugh. A violent outburst of oaths
was his answer.

"All I want to do is to git my chance at 'em.
I never missed gittin' even yet, when I laid
my mind to it."

"Sometimes you gits rather ahead of 'em I expect," said Hall.

"I b'lieve the Major bring that warrant more to git a sight at them folks 'n anything else," declared one of the party, meaning to change the subject. "He ain' keering nothin' about the little cawn them cows eat."

"He 's another one I 'll git even with," growled Pokeberry, steadying himself against a tree.

"Why n't you say that to *him?*" asked Hall. A guffaw greeted the thrust, and Pokeberry turned scowling away.

"What 's a little cawn to a man who 's got them flats?" pursued the first speaker, not heeding the interruption. "If I had them cawn-fiel's, I 'd want cows to git in thar sometimes, jes' to let me see that I did n' feel it."

"He ain' keerin' 'bout the cawn so much as 'bout the old doctor lettin' his cows keep on gittin' on him," explained the constable, in the authoritative tone of one who, holding a public office, is presumed to know whatever is necessary on every subject.

"That 's so," chimed in a tall, thin, consumptive-looking man with a red beard, whose name was Hackett. "He don' want cows nor Senators, nor nothin' else runnin' over him, an' he ain' gwine have it."

"No, that he ain'," asserted Mills. "And he jes' as live have things runnin' over him as over that lan'. He thinks as much o' that lan' o' hisn as if it was a gold mine. They ain' a acre on the place he don' think 's much of as if it was pu' low ground. He 's always talking 'bout it, an' spendin' money on it. Why, he 's spent money enough on that place to buy three plantations. He 's takin' keer of it for Bruce." The tone was dry. He was stating the fact with the air of a man who did not imagine any one would question it.

"I wonder what he 'd 'a' done if his brother had 'a' lived to divide the place with him?" said one of the crowd. "I b'lieve 't would kill him to give up a acre of that land."

"I b'lieve 't would," assented Mills. "He 's always talkin' about keepin' it in trust for Bruce."

"I ain't seen Bruce, not since he come home, but I 've heerd say he 's mighty fine and assumptious," one of the others remarked.

"He 's a mighty nice boy," said Mills. "In course, he 's kind o' curried up, but he don' put on no airs. He 's all right."

Pokeberry had returned to the group.

"D—n *him, too!* He 's another one!" he said.

"Why, you seem to be after them all to-day," laughed Hall.

"I 'm after *him*," said Pokeberry, angrily.

"You better keep some distance after him, too," said Mills. "You remember that hand-spike he hit you with when he was n't nothin' but a boy? Well, if he hits you now, you 'll think a mule 's kicked you."

Pokeberry swore inarticulately.

"I wonder if he an' the old Major sets horses any better than they used to?" Hall asked generally.

"Oh yes! the Major thinks all the worl' of him," replied Mills. "He 's talkin' about puttin' him in charge, and turnin' over ev'ything right to him. They say he 's goin' to marry a furreign lady, mighty fine an' rich. I did n't hear the Major say so," he explained.

"I heard that Bruce was gwine to manage the case for his pa to-day?" said Hall. The faint interrogation in his tone justified Mills in giving evidence of his acquaintance with the affairs of his friend.

"He is," he said, nodding his head sententiously. "He made him bring it."

The arrival of the magistrate, who was to try the case, turned the discussion into a new channel. It was Squire Johnson. The group watched the old man intently as he came around to the gate with his book—"Mayo's Guide"— under his arm.

"He's got his chance now about which he was talkin' eight or ten years ago, that evenin' you and me was here devilin' him," said Mills in an undertone to Hall.

The constable's mouth was full of tobacco. He waited a moment, then turned the quid in his mouth.

The old man bustled about with amusing self-importance, arranging his table under a tree, and laying out his book and papers; but no one paid any attention to him, for the interest of the crowd was suddenly centered on a small, black negro, who at this moment was coming up the sandy road at a slow, limping gait. He was not above five feet tall, and he wore a beaver hat of a style long obsolete, set on the back of his gray head. As he reached the outskirts of the crowd he paused, and took off his hat deferentially.

"Sarvent, marsters," he said, with a low, sweeping salaam to the crowd. The gesture had an apparent effect; for a dozen men near him returned the greeting, and the general manner towards him was one of kindness.

"Gent'men, ken you have the civility to show me which are the jestice?" he inquired with a Chesterfieldian air.

This inquiry immediately directed attention to that functionary, who came through the opening which the crowd instinctively made.

The old negro advanced.

"Jestice," he said, by way of salutation, with another of his profound bows to the portly magistrate; and then, after some search, took a letter from the lining of his old hat. He advanced a step.

"My marster have direct me to renounce that he have the honor to present you a letter."

He advanced and delivered the missive to the magistrate, whose assumed dignity in the presence of the perfectly natural and real dignity of the little negro sank at once to the point of a manifest counterfeit.

The pause in which the squire with awkward fingers was handling the note, was broken by some one inquiring of the negro as to the health of his master.

"I thank you, marster, not so very well.

140

He 's most in general uncommon indisposed. He find it impossible to repear himself on this recasion. An' he reques' me to meck his ixcuses to you, gent'men on that recount.''

This excessive mark of his master's esteem was accepted by the crowd with due dignity. The magistrate had by this time opened the letter which was written in a fine clear hand, and read its contents.

They ran as follows:

"To —— JOHNSON, Esq., *Justice of the Peace:*

"SIR: I have no defence to the action instituted against me by Charles Landon, of Landon Hall, Esq., for trespass, and I plead guilty thereto, always saving any criminal intention in the same.

"I have instructed my servant to satisfy whatever judgment you may see fit to enter against me, and should it exceed the amount he has at present, I request that no additional costs may be added other than are necessary, as I will meet whatever balance there may be by to-morrow evening.

" Resp'y your obd't serv't,

"THOMAS BROWNE."

The effect of this letter on the burly magistrate was to put him into a state of violent excitement. He read it and re-read it, and then sat down and, adjusting his spectacles, studied it carefully.

Finally, he rose and beckoning to the constable, walked out of the gate to a point across the road out of earshot of the crowd, where he proceeded to read the letter to him.

The conference was long and earnest.

"What in the —— did he have to go and plead guilty for, anyways?" he asked angrily of his friend.

"You was for him befo' you got that letter, war n't you?" inquired the constable.

"For him! In cose I was for him! You ain' s'pose I was gwine to d'cide in favor of that air overridin', slanderin' Whig, is you, not withouten I was obleeged to! I ain' forgot how he talk' about me, I tell you. I was gwine to show him who was the majistrit of this district, I was; an' I 'm gwine to yit ef they is any way to do it. What I want to know is, ain' they any way to git roun' it?" He indicated the letter.

"Read it agin," said the constable.

He read it.

" 'Savin' any criminal intention.' What do that mean?" asked the constable, shutting one eye in the effort to focus his mind on the interpretation of the abstruse words.

"That 's hit! that 's hit! What a fool I am!

Of cose, that 's hit! 'Savin' any criminal intention of the same.' He can't plead guilty without they being a criminal intention? Jim, you 's got a blame' good head on you. Ef you hed the experience, you 'd meck a first-class majistrit."

The constable looked complacent under this compliment.

"Is you heard that Sam Mills is a candidate for my place?" the magistrate asked suddenly, suspiciously.

Hall looked a little embarrassed.

"Nor; Sam ain' no candidate," he said. He turned towards the yard, perhaps to put an end to the conversation.

"You 'd meck a sight better majistrit 'n Sam," said the justice, insinuatingly. "Sam ain' got the head on him."

This commendation was received by the sub-official with becoming modesty, and the two strolled back across the sandy road, just as a horseman appeared around the curve a quarter of a mile away, approaching on a tall, handsome horse, at a slow, easy gallop. He was dressed in white linen, and carried an umbrella. The murmur of the crowd announced that he was a personage of consideration.

"There he comes," said several persons.

"That 's his horse," announced a number, more corroboratively.

The Major rode up and dismounted, flinging his bridle to a negro boy, who stepped forward with his hat off and his teeth shining. The Major raised his umbrella with deliberation. Then he came around to the gate, saluting every man he met. His manner, if a little condescending, was perfectly easy with all, and with some was cordial. It was apparent that he was highly esteemed, for the people crowded up to speak to him. His greetings evinced an accurate knowledge of each man's affairs. He even saluted politely, if a little contemptuously, the scowling justice, who, as he approached, suddenly engaged in conversation with some one, and pretended not to be aware of his arrival.

In a few minutes the magistrate took his seat, got out his silver-rimmed spectacles, wiped them carefully and put them on; cleared his mouth of tobacco, and looked at the Major, who was busy talking to one of his neighbors about his sick cow.

As no attention was paid to him, the justice called the constable, and raising his voice, ordered him to "open cote."

When this was done, by a short and incoherent proclamation, without attracting the notice of the Major, who still discoursed with an admiring group around him, the magistrate took a fresh quid of tobacco and directed the constable to inform him that his case was called. The officer, after waiting respectfully, perhaps, five minutes for a break in the Major's speech on the subject of the dry weather, delivered his message.

"Tell him I am not ready," said the gentleman, with an easy assurance, which sent the messenger back somewhat abashed, and the speech flowed on as before, only with increased urbanity.

A few moments later his overseer, with a law-book in his hand, rode up and came into the yard.

He approached his employer and waited respectfully for a time, after which he turned away to talk to some of his friends. But when the Major, after delivering himself to a group with much affability on the subject of the difference between clover and orchard-grass as a food for stock, turned suddenly and walked up to the little table beside which sat the scowling magistrate, his manager was immediately behind him.

He swept the crowd with a swift glance. He was aware that the defendant was not on the ground, and anticipating a motion for a continuance, was prepared to deliver himself with much force on the subject.

"I am ready; where is the defendant?" he asked, taking off his hat.

For answer, the magistrate leaned over, and with accentuated pomposity, handed him the note, turning his quid in his mouth, in token of his perfect indifference.

The Major's countenance fell as he read the paper. He re-read it, and then handed it back.

"I see he pleads guilty," he remarked.

"No, he don't," asserted the officer, again rolling his quid in his mouth, this time in token of his determination.

The Major frowned.

"Why, he does."

"Whar do he do it?" inquired the justice, with suspicious blandness.

"Why, there," pointing to the paper.

"I don't see it."

"Well, I know you don't; you never see anything you don't wish to see; but you would un-

146

less you were blind mentally as well as physically," asserted the irate Major, seizing the paper.

The crowd appreciated the hit, and a chuckle of enjoyment went through it. The gentleman read the note aloud, with strong emphasis. He was reading to the crowd, and they appreciated the compliment.

"Is n't that pleading guilty?" he asked, looking through his gold-rimmed spectacles.

"What does it say? 'Savin' any criminal intention in the same.' What does that mean?"

"It don't mean anything. It means that he is a word-splitting old jackass, like some other people; that 's what it means!" asserted the Major.

The crowd applauded with a guffaw.

The Major turned to them, read and re-read the paper, talked to them over it, and so berated the old magistrate, that he was thrown entirely on the defensive. He looked over at the constable for assistance; but that official had incontinently deserted and gone over to the majority, and was now grinning from ear to ear, over the Major's comments on the magistrate's judicial construction.

"If you cannot see what is written plainly

on paper, we have men among us who are less afflicted," declared the Major.

The crowd understood this to be a reference to Sam Mills, and several of them nudged him. Sam only chewed silently.

Finally, carried along by the force of his own eloquence, and inspired by the sympathy of the crowd, the Major launched out against the defendant.

"Why does he remain skulking at home when summoned by law to appear before a magistrate of this county and State?" he asked. "Why does he not come forward and defend himself like a man, if he is an honest man? Is he afraid to face daylight, that he prowls around at night, and cannot be drawn out of his hole even by process of the Commonwealth? What is he? Is he a murderer, a counterfeiter, or an abolitionist? He ought to be made to appear; he ought to be investigated. This is no longer a mere private and personal matter; his conduct is against the peace and dignity of the Commonwealth."

This, and much more to the same effect, the old gentleman delivered to the appreciative crowd, who broke into loud applause at his words.

148

When, therefore, he threw the paper on the table, and insisted that the magistrate at once try the case and give him judgment, or he would, at the next court, have an inquiry instituted as to his sanity, and see if a sane man could not be found to take his place, the justice did not have the courage to resist, and with a turn of his quid in his mouth, proceeded to try the case.

The overseer was duly sworn, and proved the facts and the amounts of estimated damages; and then the defendant was called, and failing to appear, the justice, after much figuring, gravely delivered judgment in favor of the plaintiff, for a little less than he claimed; delivering, at the same time, a speech, which was a marvel of unintelligible contradictions, attempting to reconcile his present action with the stand he had at first taken.

The contemptuous indifference with which the Major received his announcement was noted and enjoyed by the crowd. He turned to the constable.

"Levy immediately," he said. "I'll bring the old abolitionist out of his hole."

He turned away. As he did so, he was arrested by the little black pressing forward, and

149

taking off his old hat. He bowed low to the Major. His grandiloquence had disappeared, and in the presence of the gentleman he was the picture of humility.

"How much is it, marster?" he asked.

"Five dollars and thirty-seven cents," said the justice.

The negro's countenance fell.

"Dat 's mo'—" he began; then stopped; and after much fumbling, took out of his pocket an old rag wrapped about something, and carefully tied with a string. This he worked at for some time, until he had untied it. Unwrapping it carefully, he leaned over, and poured out on the table a handful of small silver and copper coins, which he carefully pushed into the very center of the table, as if fearful that they might roll off.

"Will you please count dem, marster?" he said timidly.

The coin was counted; the crowd looking on with breathless interest; the Major standing with arms folded, looking down with contemptuous amusement.

"Five dollars and twenty-five cents," said the magistrate, looking over the table, and moving every paper so as to prove that none was overlooked.

"Five dollars and twenty-five cents,—five dollars and twenty-five cents," repeated the negro to himself, looking around the table. "How much does that lack?"

After a slight calculation the amount was announced.

"Twelve cents."

This sum was wanting. The negro turned to the Major.

"Ef you could wait, marster, for about a week—?" he began.

"I won't wait," said the Major, grimly.

A pause of uncertainty ensued, in which the negro meditated. His face showed the deepest concern.

"Dat 's ev'y cent dee is on de place," he said, half audibly, to himself. Then, in a little louder tone,

"If any gent'man would lend me twelve cents?" He looked around him.

"There it is," said the Major, tossing him a dollar, and putting on his glove.

The old man's eyes gleamed as he seized the coin and laid it on the pile.

The Major walked towards the gate, but the magistrate overtook him, holding the money in one hand and a paper in the other. He stopped.

"What 's this?" he inquired impatiently.

"This is the judgment for you to mark 'satisfied'."

The old justice was glad of the opportunity to display his superior knowledge on this one point at least. The Major walked back to the table, and wrote the receipt on the paper. Then he pulled on his glove slowly, and was turning away when the justice held out to him the money. He stopped angrily, but held out his hand.

"Count it," he said shortly.

The officer counted it out coin by coin into his palm.

The Major looked at him with an ugly gleam in his eye; but just then the little negro passed by with a low salute.

"Here!" he said, and pitched the handful of money to him.

When the Major cantered out of sight, the negro was still on his knees searching in the short grass for some of the coins.

XII

ALL that afternoon a crowd remained around the little store at the Crossroads, drinking and discussing the trial. Several rows occurred; Pokeberry being concerned in more than one of them, and being the aggressor. Towards sunset he was quite under the influence of liquor, as were several others. When he was drunk he was always quarrelsome. He appeared now to have a special grudge against the Major. He came up to a group in which were Mills and Hall, and began a tirade against Major Landon for his contempt, as he charged, of a poor man. Mills took it up and denied flatly that there was any ground for such a charge.

"Any hones' po' man the Major is got as much respec' for us If he owned a big plantation and three hundred niggers," he declared. "He said once that a man as was proud of his money was like a blacksmith as bragged of the iron in his shop and did n' have sense to do any work on it."

The crowd applauded this view, and Pokeberry, enraged, growled an angry threat against the Landons.

"Why don't you go an' tell 'em so?" asked Mills. "You have mighty good opportunities, and I ain' never heard of you tellin' either of 'em."

The laugh of the crowd stung the bully, and with an oath he declared that any man was a hound who followed a Landon.

Mills was seated on the fence. He looked at him with slightly contracted eyes, but said nothing. This was accepted by Pokeberry as a sign that he was afraid of him, and he stepped a little nearer him. The crowd stopped talking and fell back. Pokeberry addressed himself directly to Mills.

"I know about you," he began.

Mills lazily let his long legs down, and slipped from the fence, which he leaned against.

"Look a-here, Pokeberry," he said slowly, with another contraction of his eyes, "go skeer runaway niggers. Don' you try it on me. If you does, runaway niggers won' have nobody to fool 'em away."

Pokeberry's answer to this was a furious demand to know what Mills meant, and a tirade against any and all persons who insinuated anything connecting him with negroes.

154

He could whip any man, he declared, who said anything connecting him with niggers.

"Look a-here, Pokeberry," said Mills, with a slight bend towards him, "talkin' 's cheap; but if you lay the weight of your hand on me, I 'll take my pocket knife and cut your throat from ear to ear."

His thin, sun-browned face was grim, and his gray eyes burnt back under his brows; but he was very quiet. There was a murmur from the bystanders. One or two of them advised Pokeberry to let him alone. Sam Mills was not a man to trifle with.

Whether it was that Pokeberry was afraid of the spare, wiry creature who looked at him with such fearless eyes, or whether he deemed it unwise to fight with such a cause of quarrel, cannot be known. But veering wholly from his former position he began suddenly an attack on Dr. Browne, whom he boldly declared to be an abolitionist. He adjourned to the little bar-room in the back of the store.

This episode broke up the crowd, and as it was sundown, Mills and the sober ones went home, leaving, however, a considerable number still hanging around the bar.

There Pokeberry continued his attack on Dr. Browne. He had sobered enough to feel that after Mills' open charge something was necessary to turn public attention from himself. He told of the disappearance of the two negroes, some years before, and charged that the old man had helped to get them away. He himself had seen him in New Orleans, he declared. He adroitly used the Major's speech of that day, with additions of his own, as a lever to move the drunken crowd.

"He 's a abolitionist," he kept on asserting, with many oaths; "and he ought to be run out. That 's what the Major said. He 's a abolitionist. He ought to be tarred and feathered, and run out,—and I am the man to do it."

By the time he had repeated this a score of times, with such embellishments as his brutal brain suggested, he had got the drunken set around him into a state in which they believed the Major had suggested the tarring and feathering and would warmly approve it. A few, with a little reason left, protested against such a lawless measure; but the majority, to the number of a dozen or more of the most worthless characters in the county, applauded.

"I 'm the man to do it," asserted Pokeberry, pulling off his coat, and turning it wrong side outwards.

A few minutes later he was out in the dark, with a drunken gang around him, clamorous to "drive the d—d abolitionist out, as the Major said."

Meantime, Major Landon had arrived at home in unusually good spirits. He had carried his point, and won his first suit; he had publicly shown that the pompous and self-important old magistrate who had long opposed him was a fool, and had held him up to open scorn and derision; and he had vindicated his rights, which were what he always contended for. Accordingly, as he mounted the long stone steps of his mansion, and turned, as he reached the top, to look back over his wide estate lying in the light of the declining sun, an expression of benignity most unusual to his firm face rested there.

The scene before him was one which might well have pleased him. As far as the eye could reach in either direction, the rolling fields, green with grain and grass, and traversed by brown fences, belonged to Landon Hall. Only immediately opposite, where the hills rose on the other side of Newfound, was a break in his domain. There was Landon Hill, the first home of his forefathers, held by an unknown stranger. There, surrounded by dense woods, and keeping himself wholly secluded, never leaving his plantation, and declining either to receive or to return visits, lived his strange neighbor. The tops of the clump of old oak trees marking the yard showed above the pines which had been allowed to grow and cover the fields, as if to conceal the old frame hip-roofed house and its surroundings from the gaze of its imposing neighbor opposite.

A slight frown crossed Major Landon's brow, as his eye rested for a moment on this spot. It was, perhaps, but the recollection of the contest he had just been through with his recluse neighbor, but with it was a deeper feeling connected with the contest in the breakfast room that morning.

The shadow passed in a moment, and he turned away and entered the wide hall.

"He 'll keep his cows to himself now, I reckon—the old abolitionist!" he said, with a half-laugh.

As his footstep sounded on the polished floor, a door on one side of the hall opened, and his wife came forward and advanced toward him with a smile of welcome. Mrs. Landon still retained much of the beauty which had made her years before the belle of her county. Yet there was a suggestion of sadness in her manner or her countenance, it could scarcely be told which, though it might have been the contrast between the white hair on her brow and the brilliant dark eyes which shone in her pale face like stars, and which, when she smiled, made her look like a girl. As she came forward with a smile to meet her husband, his whole manner changed. The gray eyes softened, the hard, strong mouth with the clean-shaven lip relaxed, and a smile lit up his face.

"Well?" she said, with a rising inflection of interrogation and of welcome.

"Oh! I won; I beat him. Routed him 'horse, foot, and dragoons.' "

He put his hat on the table; placed his gloves carefully in it; laid his horsewhip on top, and put his arm around his wife like a young lover.

"I am so glad you beat," she said; "but I hope you were not too hard on him."

"Lucy, I believe you would take up for the devil," said her husband, half-jestingly.

"Well, if he needed it, perhaps," she smiled up at him; "and really those people over there have been much in my mind of late."

"Well, I was n't hard on them at all. If I had not warranted him, there never would have been any end to it. You will bear me witness that I had stood it for years; had sent him word; and had shown the forbearance of a saint, and I was forced to apply to the law. The rascal! It is as well he did not come there, for I might have been tempted to lay my horsewhip over his shoulders. I believe he drove his cows across the river into my fields, anyhow. I do not see how they managed otherwise to get through the swamp so readily.

"I am afraid they are very poor, and you know he might have been sick when you sent him word," sighed Mrs. Landon.

"Sick! the mischief! He has not been sick for twenty years, I reckon; and he has been hiding from me that long. It is my opinion that he has been at the bottom of all the devilment that has been going on so long in the country."

"I wish they would let me do something for them," said Mrs. Landon, who was the incarnation of charity.

"I don't want to do anything for them, except get rid of them and their cows," asserted the Major. "If I had anything to go on, I would lodge a complaint against him; that is what I'd do. I hoped to have got a sight of him to-day; but the rascal was afraid to face me." The

Major was working himself up to the usual pitch of excitement over his wrongs.

"My dear, they say he is a most kind and gentle person, and does a great deal of good, and if he chooses to withdraw himself— He must be a good man; because—"

"A good man, Lucy!" interrupted the Major hotly. "Who ever heard of a good man shunning the daylight, and hiding from the eyes of his neighbors, and going out only at night like a mink or a ground-hog? He is an abolitionist, in my opinion."

When the Major expressed a thing as his "opinion," Mrs. Landon knew that there was the end of it; that it was useless to attempt to combat it, at least for the time being.

"You did not make them pay any money, I hope," she said sweetly, as she drew a chair up near that into which her husband had thrown himself.

"Of course I did n't,—that is, I gave it back after I had made him pay it," he replied. He did not think it worth while to tell her just how he had given it back. Indeed, the manner of its return did not strike him now as being altogether as praiseworthy as he had considered it when, in the presence of a gaping throng, he had tossed it disdainfully to the old negro, who had counted it out so quietly after the justice had decided against his master.

He did not know that at that moment Poke-berry Green, half sotted with liquor, was urging his word to a drunken crowd as a justification for an act of outrageous violence.

The soft evening air came through the open windows with the odor of grass upon it. It brought back a reminiscence to the Major, and he went off into reflection. Suddenly he aroused himself.

"Where is Bruce?" he asked.

"He took his rod and went off after lunch to take a fish," said Mrs. Landon, quickly. A faint shade of anxiety came into her eyes, and she looked around, taking in her husband's face in her glance.

He shifted in his chair, and presently reached over and picked up a book from the table. The act was full of emphasis. He opened the book and turned over the leaves impatiently.

"I wish he would stay at home sometimes. I don't like the way he is carrying on," he said abruptly, throwing the book back on the table, and rising with a jerk from the chair.

The look of anxiety on Mrs. Landon's face deepened.

"My dear, I hope you will not say anything to him when he comes in," she said with a tone of entreaty. "He is very—" She paused.

"Certainly not, if you wish it," said the Major; "but things have come to a pretty pass. I am to stand all his humors and disobedience and never say a word. What is he always going over there after?"

"My dear, you forget that Bruce is a man now."

"I don't care if he is forty men!" interrupted the Major, hotly; "if he stays here, he has to conform to my wishes. I thought he had improved, but I believe that he is worse than ever."

Mrs. Landon walked up and put her hand over his mouth.

"Don't say that."

"It is base ingratitude. I have given him every advantage and have spent a fortune on him, and he takes no notice of my requests— none whatever. I asked him to go up with me to-day, and—"

"He could not have understood you," defended his mother.

163

"Could not? He could not have misunderstood me; but he is bent on thwarting my wishes."

"Oh, no! I am sure that you misjudge him."

"Nothing of the kind; he was determined I should dismiss my warrant against that rascal, and when I would not, he refused to do what I asked him. Why is he suddenly so interested in that old creature? Ten days ago he was urging me to bring suit."

Mrs. Landon did not answer, hoping to put an end to the conversation; but the Major's mind was working.

"It was a great mistake to send him off to school when we did. He has got chocked full of all those fool notions about humanitarianism those people have, and which they substitute for law and order and religion and everything else. Only this morning he was talking the greatest non—"

"Oh, I don't think so; you are unjust to him," urged his wife.

"Why, he insisted that I should dismiss the warrant, and let old Browne's cows eat up my corn. What do you call that?"

"I think it was very kind and generous in him."

The Major gave a sniff.

"Kind and generous, the mischief! It's easy to be kind and generous on other people's money. It's my opinion that he is extraordinarily interested in old Browne's cows all of a sudden. The first thing you know he'll be involved in some scandal. The idea of his running opposition to Pokeberry Green!"

"I do not think there is any danger of that," Mrs. Landon said warmly.

"What makes him go down fishing every afternoon on that side of the mill-pond? He is certainly not after fish, for he never catches any."

"Oh, yes, he does," began Mrs. Landon.

"Well, in my opinion, it is not fish he's after. I will put a stop to it. I shall give him my orders, and if he wishes to stay here, he must obey them."

"You will not do any such thing," said his wife, rising, and placing her hand on his shoulder, coaxingly.

The entrance of a servant put an end to the discussion.

Whether the Major was right or not as to Bruce's general luck, he was correct about that occasion; for when Bruce returned he had not so much as one fish to show.

XIII

IF, however, Bruce had not had any good luck with fish, he had had what he deemed yet better fortune. He had met Margaret Reid again.

He was sauntering along the path which led up the pond, through the bushes and pines, when he came suddenly upon her gathering blackberries. She turned and faced him smilingly as he unexpectedly appeared.

A man may become ever so successful in after life; he may amass wealth, secure power, and achieve fame; but after a certain age he can never turn a corner in the street or a curve in the road, and meet an angel face to face with the glory of heaven all about her. This belongs to youth, and youth alone. It happened to Bruce. He turned a clump of bushes, and the dull hillside became suddenly transformed with an ineffable glory. It was only a girl with a big straw hat on her brown head, and with a glow in her cheeks, her half-startled look changing into one of pleased surprise; but she seemed to him to

"What a pity we cannot always have the thorns cut from among the flowers for us," she said.

shed a radiance around her, and to fill the woods with light.

He helped her to fill the bucket she had. He had had no idea what a charming occupation picking blackberries was. Each shining berry became a treasure and the smile that greeted his success was a reward that filled his heart. The afternoon sun shone down sultry, and the summer air was still. The not distant long-drawn lingering "Coo-coo, coo-oo-oo" of a dove was the only sound that reached them. He made Margaret sit down in the shade, and cutting some long bits of the blackberry bush filled with white blossoms pealed the briars from them for her as he lounged beside her.

Bruce had something on his conscience which he wished to tell her. Until this was done he felt uneasy. He could not, however, see his way to begin.

She took off her large hat and wreathed the boughs around it.

"What a pity we cannot always have the thorns cut from among the flowers for us," she said.

Bruce rose to his feet.

"I have something to tell you, but I do not know how to say it," he began.

167

She stood up and looked at him with grave surprise in her eyes.

"What is it?" she presently asked.

"You know that my father has brought a warrant, a suit, against your grandfather?—"

Her face flushed slightly and her eyes opened wider. He saw she knew all about it, and proceeded,

"I wish to tell you—I want you to know that it was my fault,—that it was I who made him do it,—who started it."

Her head straightened on her shoulders and her expression changed. It was plainly a shock to her.

"I wanted you to know that it was not my father. If I had known something that I now know; if I had met your old woman before, I would never have done what I did. I would make any reparation in the world I could. You don't know how much I regret it."

She suddenly turned away and began to cry quietly.

"I did not think you would have been so cruel," she sobbed. "If you knew how my grandfather has suffered—how he bears—" She could say no more.

"I do know. But I learned it too late. I regret it more than I can tell you. It was inexcusable in me.''

He took hold of her hand and kissed it.

"If you knew how deeply I regret it, you would forgive me.''

She said nothing, but she did not draw her hand away until he had kissed it again.

He had a new feeling for her, and one which he had never had before for any one. He wanted to comfort her. He longed to take her in his arms. Yet he hardly dared to touch her hand. He had suddenly grown afraid of her. What if she should be angry with him? If she should not forgive him? Life seemed to grow dark at the thought.

"Do you forgive me?'''he asked in a low voice of entreaty, as she moved slightly.

"Yes," with her face still averted.

She was wiping her eyes like a little girl. The sun once more came out. He felt like a ransomed criminal.

"I must go now," she said. "I always give my grandfather his cup of tea in the afternoon; he is so feeble, and has been so worried about that suit.''

"May I walk home with you?" He asked it as if she had the power of life and death.

She allowed him to walk as far as the spring. He felt grateful for even this, and followed her humbly.

At the spring she said good-by, and held out her hand.

He took it and pressed it; and then, raising it quickly, pressed it reverently to his lips.

"Good-by."

She gave a little start, and drew away.

He did not dare to look at her. When he did look up, her face was still turned away from him, and she moved towards the path which led up to the house. It was all that he could do not to rush after her and, seizing her in his arms, pour out his heart to her. As he walked home the whole earth seemed to have become but a setting for that slim girl the other side of the river.

When Bruce reached home, he was too much filled with thoughts of Margaret Reid to care for other company. He did not care to meet his father, who he knew would be full of his case. So he sauntered into the library, and pretended to look over a book; but he found himself unable to read, and he was sinking into a drowsy state of insensibility to everything around him, when he was aroused by a rapid step outside, followed by a quick knock on the door.

"Come in," he called. He had some curiosity; for it was not often in that placid atmosphere that any step so energetic was heard, or any rap so excited.

A servant entered, and shutting the door behind him, stopped, hat in hand. He was manifestly under unusual excitement.

"Well, Henry, what is it?" inquired his master.

"I heah dee's some trouble gwine on over on the other side of the pawn," he began hesitatingly, "and I thought I'd better come and let marster know."

"Yes, that's right," said Bruce, languidly. "What is it?"

"I don' know, suh. Dick—Dick Runaway's jes' come home,—he's been off two or three days,—an' he heah somehow about de warrant-tryin' to-day, an' he say he heah dat after marster come away dee all got to drinkin' at de groggery, an' dat Pokeberry got 'em sort o' stirred up, an' dat Dick Runaway say dee's gone over to old Dr. Browne's to breck him up,—to tar an' feather him, an' burn his house down."

Bruce sprang to his feet.

"What 's that?" he asked sharply. "A mob! Why have they gone there?"

"I don' know, suh. Dick says dee 's a whole parcel on 'em," said the negro, looking down at the side of his shoe. "He say he heah 'em talkin', an' dee say 't is cause he 's a 'abolitioner,' or some 'n'; I don't know nuthin' 'bout it." He gave a sort of uneasy laugh at the word. "Dat feller Pokeberry 's a bad feller," he added.

"All right," said Bruce; "I 'll see about it. That 's all."

He turned and hurried to his room, and the negro retired.

A minute later Bruce left the house by a side door, with his shot-gun in his hand, and descended the hill towards the river at a swift trot.

XIV

WHEN Margaret had given her grandfather his tea, she went to her room. Somehow she was filled with a mysterious unrest. What had come over her? She did not know herself. For the first time the life she was leading failed to satisfy her; she was stifled and confined. She had suddenly outgrown her surroundings and become miserable.

Why did her grandfather remain shut up? she thought! Why had he always discountenanced her going out into the neighborhood? Why was he so silent about her mother? Why was he so strange sometimes? Oh, if he should die and leave her! Why were they so secluded? Had he been rich once? The old dresses in the trunks in the garret were of the finest stuffs. Whose could they have been? Why was she suddenly so dissatisfied and wretched? And, oh! why was she thinking at all of Bruce Landon? He was nothing to her. He must be infinitely above her. She knew he was; yet she did not feel it. He had kissed her hand. Why had he done it? He had taken a liberty with her, and she had permitted it, and now he despised her. She felt sure of it. She despised herself. She would never see him again. Yes, she would go and meet him, and show him that she was not one to be kissed and taken liberties with. She was so wretched that she ended by throwing herself on her bed and crying herself to sleep. When she awakened, it was nearly dark. Her grandfather was calling her.

There was a lovely, old curious-flowered lawn, with short sleeves and a short waist. She had brought it down from the garret, and had tried it on. It just fitted her. It had lain in her dresser ever since. She took it out and, under an impulse, put it on. It was the first time she had worn anything but the plain stuff bought in the country. To match it she coiled her abundant hair and piled it high on her head in the quaint style which she had seen in the pictures of the ladies who wore such gowns. She could not help being pleased at the result. If Bruce Landon could only see her in it! She determined to surprise her grandfather.

"All right; I 'm coming in a moment," she called cheerfully to him, in answer to his impatient summons.

When she walked in, the old man nearly sprang from his chair. She was a vision.

"Gracious God! where did you get that?" he gasped.

She told him. He sank back in his chair and closed his eyes. A groan escaped his pale lips.

"What is it, grandpapa?" she asked, frightened at the effect on him.

"Nothing; only you startled me," he said. She pressed him.

"I have made you an outcast, I have sold your birthright," he said bitterly. "You will live to curse me."

"Oh, grandpapa!" She kissed him tenderly. "You are my all—all I have in the world."

"Yes, all—all you have in the world; and when I have gone, what will you have? It is the same with every one. I seem to have cursed them all, to have put a blight upon them. I have been cursed."

He was speaking to himself.

"Oh, grandpapa, please don't!" sobbed Margaret, putting her hands on him caressingly.

"I have been your worst enemy," groaned

175

the old man. "If you knew all, you would curse me."

Margaret knelt beside him and flung her arms around him.

"I would love you as I do, better than all the world."

"I hoped you would escape," he muttered, his head sinking back on his pillow.

"Grandpapa, tell me about my mother," she pleaded, laying her hand on his shoulder.

He became too agitated to do so. But after a time he grew calmer.

"She was an angel," he said. And then he told her her story.

He had not understood her, and had been too hard with her; had opposed her marriage to a young officer, whom she loved, and she had married him against his wishes. He was killed shortly afterwards. But even then, he had been cruel and had refused to forgive her. Then she, Margaret, had been born, and she had sent for him to come and forgive her before she died, and he had gone to her, and reached her just in time. She had died in his arms, forgiven; after she had placed her baby in his hands in token of her love for him. He had resigned from the navy, bought this place, and come here to live.

At the end he sank back on his pillow and closed his eyes with a groan.

It was the first time he had ever said so much of her, and the girl's hungry spirit was feeding on the details and memories the old gentleman recalled, as if they were the bread of life.

"Grandpapa, was she beautiful?" she asked.

"As an angel," he said gravely. "She was very like you, my darling. She was fitted to shine in any station." The current of his thoughts seemed to change.

"Margaret," he said suddenly, "you have met that young man—young Landon?"

"Yes, grandpapa," in a very low voice. She was glad the twilight shielded her.

"He is proud and vain of his name and position?" There was an interrogation rather than an affirmation in his tone.

"I do not know—I cannot tell."

"He is handsome? and self-confident?" Again the interrogation.

Her heart gave a bound at the picture the terms called up.

"Yes, grandpapa—exceedingly."

"It is the way with all of them," he murmured. "It is the curse. You love him?"

"No, grandpapa," with a little gasp.

"You will fall in love with him," said the old gentleman, this time without the interrogation in his tone. "And he will not fall in love with you—" he paused, "unless,— unless—" He broke off. "You will live to curse me," he said bitterly. "I am cursed. I have always been." His head sank on his breast.

The girl flung herself on her knees beside him, and, stretching out her arms, placed her hands on his shoulders and held him.

"Grandpapa," she said, eagerly lifting her face, "I am not in love with him; I will never be in love with him without your full approval. I promise you here on my knees. Oh, Grandfather! Her voice broke. She laid her face against him and began to sob. A moment later she raised up. "I am your grand-daughter," she said with pride, "and I will never be in love with him—unless he is first in love with me, and then not without your consent." She rose and seated herself calmly in her chair.

A look of admiration came over the old man's face that brought back a spark of the fire of youth.

"He will be in love with you," he said, as if to himself.

Suddenly both started, as a strange noise came to them from without.

Any sound was a novelty in that quiet spot, where even the cackling of a hen, the low of the cows, or the voices of the birds made themselves felt and noted on the utter silence of the place.

But this noise was peculiar: it was confused, unwonted, threatening.

Margaret's eyes opened wide as she sat straight upright in her chair, and turned her head to the window. The noise swelled. Suddenly a gun was fired without, and loud shouts, mingled with boisterous laughter, sounded in the yard. Margaret sprang to her feet, with a white face, and her grandfather suddenly rose from his chair, under the excitement of the moment oblivious of his rheumatism, and started to the door.

"Youee—yah—ah!" came the shouts from without, followed by loud, boisterous laughter; and then high above it all came the shrill, excited voice of old Milly, the words drowned by the confusion and derision which greeted them. Margaret pressed close to her grandfather.

"Oh, grandfather! what is it coming? Who

are they? What can they want? Don't go out,
—please," as the old man started to the door.

Old Milly's voice suddenly rang out,

"Ole marster."

The effect was electrical. The old officer
turned back, and, reaching up over the mantel,
seized the dusty sabre which had hung there for
many a long day, and strode towards the door.
Before he could reach it, however, the outer
door, which always remained unlocked, was
flung open, and a number of intruders crowded
pell-mell into the narrow hall with shouts and
oaths.

"Come out of your hole, you old abolitionist!" they cried.

Margaret started to spring to the door of the
chamber to lock it, but before she could reach
it, it was thrown open violently, disclosing a
coarse, burly fellow, his face blackened as a
disguise, and with a long, charred pine torch in
his hand, as heavy as a club; whilst behind him
were a half-a-dozen others, also with blackened
faces, and all evidently full of liquor.

The girl shrank back with a cry of terror as
the ruffian in front broke into a loud laugh and,
calling to those behind to come on, stepped in
at the door. The old surgeon, with a quick move-

ment, put the girl behind him, and seizing the weapon in both hands, jerked the sword from the rusty scabbard. Youth had suddenly come back to his veins; the emaciated frame straightened, and the sunken eyes blazed like coals. An angry exclamation burst from his lips, and he took a step forward, about to dash upon the mob. But Margaret, in her terror, was clinging to him and holding him. As it was, the ruffians gave back at the sudden transformation and retreated almost out of the room. They stood thus, for a moment, blocking the door. Then the blackened-faced leader called once more to his comrades to come on, and with drunken bravado advanced again into the apartment, cursing his companions for not backing him. They were just closing up again, when something occurred outside which drove the leaders confusedly several steps into the room, and so close to the old man as he stood at bay, that he raised his sword with a furious oath to cut the leader down.

Before he could do so, however, the mob which blocked the door was suddenly split, and a young fellow burst through them, flinging them right and left. He was bareheaded, and in one hand he grasped a shot-gun. As he sprang into the room and faced about, the mob fell back, squeezing out of the door as fast as they could, for it was Bruce Landon, with his Landon blood up and a gun in his hand.

"Get out of here, you ruffians!" he said, bringing his gun down upon them. They did not need this. They were getting out as fast as they could, all, at least, except the leader, who was Pokeberry Green.

With the bravado born of his brutal nature inflamed by liquor, he turned and jerked out a pistol. As he did so, however, Bruce sprang on him. The impetus of the leap sent him spinning out into the passage, where, in the dark, they wrestled and struggled for life.

Bruce was unable to use one hand well, as he still held his gun; but he had driven Pokeberry to the door and was forcing him steadily back when there was a deafening report, a sudden blaze of light in his face, and he felt a sensation as if a hot needle had run into his shoulder. He sank back, letting go his antagonist; but mustering all his strength, swung his gun around his head with his uninjured arm and gave him a blow which sent him staggering backward, out into the darkness. He heard him fall heavily on the portico, and then he remembered no more.

The next thing he knew, he felt a soft touch on his arm and was conscious that his shoulder hurt him a good deal, and that he was violently thirsty. Some one was saying something in a low voice, and he opened his eyes. He was lying on a bed with white curtains around it, in a little, low-pitched room. One arm was bare, and his shoulder was being bandaged by two persons, one of whom was an old man, with a long, white beard and eyes set far back under his heavy brows, who was sitting on the bed; and the other, a young girl, who was kneeling beside him, with her face nearly on a level with his. Her hands were busy with the bandages, one on his arm and one holding the roll. Her face was very grave and solicitous. When he first opened his eyes her dark lashes were almost lying on her cheek, as she looked down at her work. As he moved, however, she glanced at his face, and as she caught his gaze, her great dark eyes suddenly lit up, lighting her whole face. Bruce never forgot the look, nor the sensation of her soft hand on his arm.

"I must get up," he said immediately; but both voices, at once, insisted that he must do nothing of the kind; the old man, with grave decision, and the girl, with sweet earnestness. As Bruce was feeling weak, he sank back and languidly gazed at the two or three old slender chairs, and the thin-legged table, on which were a few books, and a bowl filled with jonquils, which shone like gold against the snowy drapery of the dresser beyond.

XV

BRUCE'S wound proved, after all, not to be serious; and he walked home next day, though he was pallid and feeble from loss of blood.

Bruce, however, would not have cared how long he had to remain a patient in that hospital. His hours of convalescence were all too brief. They were hurried by the presence of a nurse who would have made any pain endurable and any languors sweet. As she came in and out, her slim hands bearing some dainty dish prepared by the old colored mammy under her direction, and Bruce dared hope with her aid, her face in its serene gravity a study on which the young man could exhaust his imagination, he blessed the shot that had brought him there, and gave himself up to his dreams. Was ever a man so blessed! Was ever a nurse so dainty, so beautiful and so bewitching! He feigned to be in pain only to have a shadow of sympathetic suffering flit across that snowy brow with the brown hair growing there in such tender curves, and to be weaker than he was only to have her arrange his pillow and smooth his coverlid. She was Saint Theresa and Saint Ursula in one, in fact, she was just a beautiful young saint, more lovely and more holy than all that legend told of and he canonized her in his heart, selfishly rejoicing that she was only his.

Margaret, on her part, had her dreams also. Had he not come like a Heaven-sent angel to aid them in the hour of their need—a Paladin like one of old who with his single arm had protected them and driven out the horde of ruffians who might have sacked their house! Was ever such courage, such prowess! She pictured to herself over again the vision of his first appearance in that dreadful hour when he stood facing the mob with blazing eyes and tense, proud face in which anger and courage and resolution all flamed. Then that other picture came when with white face proud and resolute even in its unconsciousness he lay on the floor at her feet and she thought he was dead.

At the memory she grew more tender and fancied some sudden need that she might have the happiness of ministering to him.

As Bruce, after a little, found himself stronger his nurse was transformed into a companion, and Bruce had a novel experience. He discovered in her a new charm. Margaret's secluded life had largely cut her off from association with others of her age and had thrown her for companionship largely on her reading and her reflections. As a result she was interested rather in things than in persons and her conversation instead of being confined to petty personalities like that of most of her kind and age was rather of higher things. Bruce unexpectedly became aware that he was talking to some one who had really thought and had ideas of her own. He found himself in the presence of intellect and recognized that it was necessary to use his intellect if he wished to hold his place in her esteem. To find a girl who was prompt in her judgment that "The Rape of the Lock" was a better poem than the "Essay on Man," and that "The Heart of Midlothian" was a finer novel than "Ivanhoe" and was prepared to back up her judgment with sundry sound reasons, was sufficiently novel in the young man's experience. And when she touched on nearer and more practical matters, he was even more astonished. He had inherited most of his opinions as he had inherited his religion. He had accepted them without really thinking about them. To find a young girl questioning them and seriously thinking of the reasons for things which he had always assumed to be unquestionable astonished him and startled him somewhat. Hitherto he had never thought of a girl but as a beautiful thing to admire, to protect and to love; an ornament of life, a flower for a man to wear and enjoy. But here was some one who was wholly new to his experience. Here was intellect as well as beauty. Also here were ideas so novel that they surprised and mystified him. Where could she have gotten her notion which she stated so simply that slavery was not a perpetual nor a divine institution and that it would some day be abolished and all the negroes be free! This was in direct variance with all the teaching Bruce had ever received. Of course, he knew that there was a growing element in the North, who, now that they had gotten rid of their own slaves, wanted to take the slaves from the Southerners, but under that, as he had always heard, was sheer envy and, even there the great body of the people recognized the rights of the South. Did not the Bible teach slavery?—St. Paul and all of them?

"Well, if it did," said this serene-faced little philosopher, "it must have been only as a human institution which was allowed rather than inculcated. St. Paul had to take a good many things as he found them—and the great teaching of the church was for a new and moral life. The good God has told us to love Him with all our heart and soul and mind, and our neighbor as ourself, and this cannot be with slavery. You would not want any one to hold you in slavery?''

It crossed the young man's mind as his eyes rested on the earnest face before him with its delicious coloring, the eyes full of light, the face glowing with earnestness, that there might be a slavery which he might find endurable and that its soft chains were fast binding him; but she was too serious to allow changing the subject and with a smile which was half a sigh, at putting by so fair an opportunity, he maintained that there was a great difference between a white man and others. He found his argument a little upset by her observation that the slavery St. Paul had mentioned was that of white people.

Then Bruce being driven from one line of defence resorted to an argument not unusual with men.

''But, you have slaves?'' he began—

''They are not mine,'' she said quietly, ''and

189

they know that whenever they wish it they can go.''

''Some of ours go anyhow—we have an incorrigible runaway. He has even gotten the name of Runaway Dick from his love of freedom.''

''I know him,'' said the girl. ''Why do you not set him free?''

''Oh! he is free enough. He goes off whenever he likes—but how on earth did you come to know him?'' He thought of Dick's having brought the news of the attack on them by the mob.

''Oh! he has been here once or twice to get food or medicine when he was sick—''

''Do you not know that it is breaking the law to give food or shelter to a runaway?'' laughed Bruce.

''No, I did not. Is it? Then I think it a meritorious act to evade such an iniquitous law,'' she said warmly, her eyes lighting up.

''I think so, too. You need not look at me that way. In fact, Dick is free in all but name. As for that matter, most of our negroes are.''

''That is the trouble—there is a wide difference between the two. Have you ever read 'Uncle Tom's Cabin'?'' she asked suddenly.

''No. I would not read such a book. It is a

190

travesty of Southern life—a jumble of libels on the South.''

"How do you know that if you have never read it?"

"I have heard so. Every one says so. Why when it came out a few years ago all the papers took it up and discussed it and they all agreed."

"I think a man ought to form his own judgment on matters and not take the opinions formed by others. A girl may have to accept opinions formed for her, for she may not have an opportunity to form her own opinions and then her mistakes do not reach so far—But if I were a man!"

Bruce winced. The flashing eyes and little hand grown suddenly tense were very persuasive.

"Of course, I shall read it," he said grandly. "Did you find it interesting?"

"Intensely. It gives a dreadful picture of slavery in the far South; of evils which exist in spite of the efforts of kind masters and mistresses everywhere. My grandfather says it has rung the knell of slavery."

"Why, old Mr. Strang preaches that slavery is not only of divine origin; but will exist in the millennium," said Bruce laughing.

"How can he be so wicked and so foolish!" exclaimed Margaret. "As if he knew the intentions of the good God!"

"Well, he is not very wise, I grant," defended Bruce with a vivid recollection of many dreary hours spent on a hard pew under his sonorous ministrations; "but he certainly is not wicked. He is one of the best men in the world and even you could not be more kind in your practical application of the golden rule."

"I think that a man is accountable for his teachings," persisted the girl, "and often what a man says is more lasting than his actions—especially in the pulpit."

"I do not know about that. Mr. Strang's life is certainly his best sermon. Once when he broke through a bridge and all his sermons got wet, my father said that no great harm was done for they 'd all get dry again."

The girl laughed, and further discussion was interrupted by the entrance of her grandfather, who came to see how the patient was.

"What are you doing disobeying my orders?" he said with a smile to his grand-daughter. "Did I not caution you against tiring him?"

Bruce's assertion that he was not only not

tired but was improved by the conversation, certainly had the merit of sincerity.

"Well, I think you are doing very well—very well indeed," said the old man, "and they have sent over for you from—your home."

Bruce's heart sank. Had he to leave that asylum—that nurse? For a fraction of a second his feeling against his assailant of the evening before was regret that his bullet had not gone a shade deeper. He glanced at Margaret. She had turned and was looking out of the window, so that he could not see her face; but he hoped from her attitude that she was sorry to have him leave.

"Tell them I will walk home," he said. There was a little demurring on the old surgeon's part, and Margaret began to protest warmly; but Bruce was determined to show that he was not a milksop and the Doctor yielded, admitting that he did not think the walk would hurt him.

There was intense excitement at Landon Hall when next morning the fact that he had been shot was known, even though it was reported that the wound was not at all serious. His father was in a consuming fury. He vowed that he would at once have the entire gang of ruffians arrested and sent to the penitentiary. He was only restrained by the knowledge that to do this it would be necessary to bring out the fact of Bruce's presence on the occasion; and this he was unwilling to do. He could not tolerate the idea of his name being dragged into public in connection with one whom he detested. This, however, did not prevent his publicly denouncing the affair in terms little short of violent.

That such an outrage should have been perpetrated in his immediate neighborhood, under his very nose, and, as it were, actually on the borders of his own plantation, was a crime not to be overlooked. The Major had no conception that his words had borne a part in the instigation of the act: they had been spoken in heat, and he had never given a thought to them since. Indeed, he could not have been induced to believe that any connection existed between them and the outrageous act which had been perpetrated. Words were one thing,—every man had a right to talk and express his opinion; but to go and break into a man's house in the night, and attempt to drag him out—why, it was monstrous! He would have gone over to Dr. Browne's and have advised him to have the whole set of ruffians arrested, but he had sworn that he would never set his foot on the place until he owned it. He contented himself, therefore, with riding about the neighborhood, denouncing the whole affair with all the vigor of a somewhat picturesque vocabulary, and threatening to go to court himself and have every scoundrel in the party indicted.

Indeed, more than once he found some of the perpetrators as he believed, and gave his opinion of their act in such forcible terms that they slunk away with blanched faces. Pokeberry, he publicly affirmed, ought to be hanged, and he openly prophesied that he would be, only expressing his fear that some untoward accident might cheat the gallows out of its due.

The old gentleman was at heart intensely pleased at Bruce's rescue of his neighbors, and behind his back referred to his courage and decision as having held at bay a large mob and as having been worthy of a Landon.

This, however, did not prevent him from being very scornful to Bruce himself about his sudden appearance at "old Browne's" and his engaging in a disreputable brawl, when, not long subsequently, he found Bruce, one afternoon, with his arm still in a sling, returning from that side of the stream, without even the time-worn excuse of a fishing-rod. He flung a caustic gibe at him about engaging in permanent rivalry with his friend Pokeberry. Bruce's face, which had flushed with self-consciousness on coming unexpectedly on his father, turned a sudden white. He was in no mood for jesting; for he had been waiting and watching in vain all the long afternoon in the hope of catching a glimpse of the face which now never left his mind during his waking hours. He started to reply; but by a strong effort controlled himself, and, turning away, walked home.

The Major, on reaching the house, sought his wife and held a long interview with her. He would as soon not have confessed his shortcomings to the Deity as to his wife. As a result of this conference he, after tea, sent for Bruce, and had a short interview with him. It began inauspiciously; for both were heated at the start. In the first place, Bruce knocked at the door of the library, where his father was. This offended the old gentleman, who was in a mood in which he might have been offended if he had not knocked.

"You are formal," he said coldly, as the young man entered, and remained standing.

"I thought it was a formal interview to which I was invited, sir," said Bruce, with marked dignity.

"It depends upon you," said the Major. "Take a seat; I wish to speak to you."

He came to the point quickly.

"Bruce," he said, "I want you to go abroad."

The young man started. Go abroad, and never see Margaret Reid again!

His father continued:

"I want you to go abroad at once. I will give you all the money you wish to spend, and you can be as independent as you please. You already have many pleasant acquaintances in England and France; and I feel sure that I can secure for you a position as secretary with one of the legations,—perhaps, in one of those countries. It will furnish you something to do, and give you official position."

He ended, and looked at Bruce hopefully. He had got through better than he had expected.

"I am very much obliged to you," said Bruce, with great urbanity. "But I don't want to go."

The Major's calm forsook him.

"Well, sir, I order you to go."

"May I ask, sir, why you propose to take me up and banish me like an exile? Why not shut me up on a *lettre de cachet?*" inquired the young man.

"Yes, sir, you may. It is because you are throwing away your life in an idle, worthless fashion; associating with people who are not fit associates for a gentleman; consorting with an unknown young woman; making yourself the talk of the country, and dragging your name, which is an honorable one, into the vulgar gossip at every Crossroads groggery in the neighborhood!" His sentences were shot out one after the other.

Bruce sprang to his feet.

"It is not true," he said angrily; then qualified it. "You are not speaking of your own knowledge; and whoever has informed you has said what is false. Miss Reid is a lady—"

"Not so, sir," retorted the Major. "It is true, and I do speak of my own knowledge: even the negroes are talking about it. It is a disgrace; and whether you go to Europe or not, I forbid you ever to go again to that place. You cannot be going to marry the young woman, and I will not stand any disgrace. If I hear of you doing anything disgraceful I will cut you off with a shilling. What is more, I will not have my name dragged into the mire of low scandal-mongering, and if you go again, you go at your peril.'' He turned to leave.

Bruce's face turned white.

''You do not know what you are talking about. I am a gentleman.''

The Major made a gesture.

''I refuse to be dictated to as if I were a negro,'' said the young man. ''I will go wherever and whenever I please.''

''At your peril.''

The Major, without awaiting his answer, left the room, leaving him to reflect on his words.

The next morning the Major mounted his horse and rode down upon the river, with an expression on his face which bespoke something extraordinary. He was dressed in immaculate linen from throat to heel, and carried a light umbrella. His face above his high collar was unusually severe. Everything that he saw was wrong. His overseer told him ''that fellow Dick Runaway'' had gone off again the night before, the second time in three months. He ''ought to sell him; he could not do anything with him.'' He ''believed that old man over across the pond hired him to take care of his cows; knew he harbored him." The Major was inclined to believe so too, but scouted the notion to the overseer. He was not agreeing with any one just then. However, he vowed he would not stand Dick any longer. He would not have a runaway negro. He would sell him as soon as he was caught.

The overseer was so elated that he made a slip. He did n't know anybody who could catch him except Pokeberry; should he tell Pokeberry to go after him?

The mention of Pokeberry touched the Major into flame.

Pokeberry! that scoundrel! No; he hoped if he went after Dick, Dick would kill him; he would spend every dollar of his estate defending him if he did. He had brought him home once tied like a calf in a butcher's wagon, the inhuman scoundrel. He would rather never have Dick back, rather lose every negro on his place, than have that ruffian go after him again.

He left the overseer speechless and over-whelmed.

After finding fault with everything he saw, he rode up the river, through the woods. It was spring, and the trees were still fresh and tender, their varied tints looking in the landscape like vast flowers. The old road, so long unused, was in many places grown up in bushes, the leafy limbs meeting across the path, so that the Major, to pass under them, had frequently to lean down on his bay horse's neck. Still he pushed on, and it was only when he came to the narrow ford across the stream at the head of the pond that he paused.

There he stopped, irresolute. The old carriage-way down to the stream on his side and up on the other had been washed into two cuts; but they were covered with old leaves, and a spreading dogwood filled with snowy bloom was growing right in the middle of the cut. The Major looked across. He had not passed that boundary for fifteen years. On the other side, the track was even less distinct than on his; for young pines were growing up in it. He looked beyond the stream, and then, as if undecided, glanced back in the direction from which he had come. Suddenly he tightened the rein, and giving the hesitating horse the whip, rode down to the water, went floundering through the narrow, miry stream, and pushed on up the long-unused track. The struggle that it had cost to bring him across had brought a cloud on the Major's face; his brows were knit, and now, as he walked his horse along, his look was grim enough. To think that this was the home of his fathers, the cradle of his race; held by an alien; allowed to grow up in a wilderness; worse than any poor white's place! It was enough to make his father turn in his grave. Why, those blackguards were right,—were almost right,—had some excuse for trying to drive him off. If he were not an abolitionist, he was worse. And to think of his son stooping to be in love with this man's granddaughter! It was a disgrace! He could not sustain the thought of it. He would cut him off with a shilling if he ever set foot on the place again. Things had gone too far. He would stand no more! Pines everywhere! He would see the young woman and settle the matter for good and all. She would hardly fail to accede to his wishes; few could. If she did,—if she was brazen, why, he would buy her off.

He passed over the hill through pines all the way, and beyond where the fence used to be. It was all rotted now, and he rode on through the thicket towards the house. Just as he arrived in sight of an opening some distance ahead, which he knew must be the yard, he came in view of some one walking along the path before

him,—a young woman. A large straw hat concealed her head, and she carried a basket on her
arm. She was tall and evidently young, and it
occurred to the Major, as he did not know her,
that she was some visitor. Hearing his horse,
she turned hastily and looked back, but was too
far distant for him to see her face; then she
quickened her step. The Major, wishing to get
her to bear a message, pushed his horse to a trot
to overtake her. He came up to her just as she
reached the rude "bars" of small unbarked pine
poles, which, to keep the cows in, were thrown
across the road between the two old gate-posts
which had once formed the entrance to the yard.

"I say,—good morning," said the Major, sitting in an easy posture on his handsome bay and
gazing ahead at the old house which could just
be seen through the trees. He did not even look
at her.

"Can you take a message for me to the young
woman in there,—Dr. Browne's grand-daughter, Miss Browne, or whatever her name is?"

"I am Dr. Browne's grand-daughter," said
the young woman, in a placid, melodious voice,
turning up to him a face a little flushed with the
excitement of the unexpected meeting; but with
calm, dark eyes under straight black brows, and

with a certain look which the Major thought of afterwards and which made him forget all else.

"Oh! ah! ah! You don't say so! I beg your pardon, I 'm sure," he began, and before he knew it he had dismounted and was standing down on the ground with his hat in his hand.

How awkward it was, and how like a fool he felt! Why, she was a beauty and quite a lady. What the deuce should he say!

"It is a very fine day—ah!" he began, wishing himself at home, or in perdition, or anywhere but where he was.

"Yes, I have been enjoying it," she said placidly, looking him full in the eyes, her face a little lifted and slightly flushed, her eyes wide, and her lips the least bit compressed.

How melodious her voice was! Quite like a lady's voice, thought the Major. He made a remark about the flowers she had in her basket, rather to gain time and avoid coming to the point than because they pleased him particularly. He was embarrassed by finding her so different from what he expected, so self-possessed, and undeniably beautiful.

"Yes?" with a rising inflection. She looked down at them gravely, and reaching her hand around instinctively arranged them in the basket. Then she looked at him inquiringly.

He was embarrassed by finding her so different
from what he expected.

There was no hope for it; he must go on.

"I—I—. If you will allow me, I will put on my hat; the sun is a little warm," he said, faltering.

She bowed.

"Certainly."

"I—I—I came to speak to you about my son," began the Major, and paused.

Her face flushed a little, and she drew in her breath in a startled way, the lips growing just a shade more compressed.

He looked away, and then growing angry with himself, began rapidly.

"I want to say something to you about my son, Mr. Bruce Landon?"

There was a shade of interrogation in his tone, and she bowed slightly to show that she understood him. She was standing very straight.

"My son is—is a gentleman—" He paused, abashed at his speech.

"Damnably unlike his father on this present occasion," he thought suddenly, almost amused at the reflection. Then he added in a softer tone,

"He is my only son, and—I—I have plans for him, and I wanted—" He paused.

"Yes?" she bowed inquiringly, still looking

him full in the face with that embarrassing, un-flinching gaze from her eyes.

"I don't want you to marry him," blurted out the Major, desperately.

"Neither do I. You need have no fear; I have no idea of marrying him," she said quietly, never taking her eyes from his face. Her head straightened on her shoulders just a little.

The Major almost staggered. She refuse Bruce! His son! Impossible!

"He is my only son, and I have made plans for him," explained the Major again lamely, in impotent contempt for himself.

"I will not prevent your carrying them out," she said, raising her head perceptibly, and standing more erect than she had done. "I will never marry him."

"You are far too good for him," he began, feeling that some amend was to be made her. "I regret having to say what I have done—" he was going on; but the girl drew herself up, and, without taking her eyes from his face, said,

"You know nothing about me." Then as the Major paused abashed, added, still in the same modulated voice,

"Is that all?"

"Yes," said the Major, in a crestfallen tone, gathering up his bridle-reins.

"I am sorry—" he began, but again her look stopped him. He dared not apologize.

She backed slightly away. It might have been to get out of the reach of his horse; but it seemed to the Major as if a queen were ending an audience.

"Good-by. I am very much obliged to you," said the old gentleman, in a rather subdued tone, putting on his hat and turning to mount.

"Good day." She turned and walked slowly towards the house.

The Major rode off at a gallop, feeling more contempt for himself than he ever had done in his life.

Who was she like?

XVI

THE Major had pulled in his horse and was riding through the pines in deep reflection, when a large man stepped suddenly out of the thick growth beside the way into the narrow path just before him, facing him. The sudden apparition caused the spirited horse that the Major rode to bound and half wheel around; but the practised hand on the bridle brought him back. It was Pokeberry Green, and as usual he carried his long, double-barrelled gun in the hollow of his left arm. He stood, glowering, right in the middle of the road.

The Major's anger rose.

"What do you mean, sir, by jumping out of the bushes in that manner in front of a gentleman's horse? Have you no sense left? Get out of the way, and let me come by."

"I want to see you," growled Pokeberry.

"Well, it 's more than I do you. What do you want to see me about?"

"I hear," he began angrily, "that you said I was in that mob that went t'other night to old man Browne's and broke in his house?" His manner was very threatening, and he looked thoroughly dangerous.

"Well, you heard right," said the Major, boldly; "I did say so. And I said furthermore that you ought to be prosecuted and sent to the penitentiary, and I will have it done if you don't look out. It's an outrage that such a scoundrel should be allowed to run free. You are a disgrace to the neighborhood."

The man with an angry oath suddenly cocked his gun, and, flinging it a little forward, started to raise it.

If the Major had quailed ever so little, murder would have been done on the spot. But he did not. The menacing act of the ruffian simply enraged him. Intrepidly pushing his frightened horse closer up to him, he raised his whip.

"Lower that gun instantly, you scoundrel!" he said. "Do you think I am to be threatened? If you dare to assault me in this way, I'll have you tied to a tree and thrashed within an inch of your life."

The absolute fearlessness of the old gentleman, and his imperious anger, overwhelmed the ruffian. His eyes quailed and fell, and, dropping his gun, he stepped back out of the way.

"I ain' threatenin' nobody," he half growled, half whined. "I been squirrel-huntin', an' I jes' wanted to tell you I did n' had nothin' to do with that there thing t'other night. I 'll swar on a stack of Bibles I did n', and I can prove it by a hundred witnesses. I hope I may die on the spot if I wan' home sleep by sundown. I was home drunk that evening," he added corroboratively.

"I have no doubt that you can prove it by the other scoundrels who were there," said the implacable Major, "who will quite willingly swear to that or any other invention you may suggest; but if you expect to get off by that, I tell you now that you are mistaken. There is some law left in the land, I hope; and unless you find it so, my name is not Landon."

So saying, he passed on, leaving the crestfallen and subdued Pokeberry cursing him under his breath, and looking dangerously at his black gun-barrels.

He had not gone over a quarter of a mile further and had not quite reached the river, when his horse again started and shied in the narrow track. The Major angrily faced him towards the point from which he had veered, thinking, perhaps, that Pokeberry had intercepted him. With pointed ears and high head the horse backed away. His master looked earnestly into the woods.

"Walk out from behind that tree, and come here!" he suddenly called sternly, to an invisible person.

Finding himself discovered, a negro stepped out, and came slowly and humbly towards him. He was apparently about thirty years of age, tall and strongly built, and very black.

"My marster," he said.

The Major pitched into him with volubility. Dick's spirits rose; for it was Dick Runaway himself. He recognized in his master's manner a by no means dangerous mood. It was when he was stern and silent that he was to be feared.

"What do you run away for?" finally demanded the Major. "I rescued you once and you swore solemnly that you 'd never run off again. Do you think that I have nothing to do but support a worthless, runaway vagabond, who lives half his time in the woods? I believe that you have lived half your life in the woods. What did you run away for this time?"

The negro stood looking down on the ground in some embarrassment. Suddenly he broke off a long, stout dogwood switch from a thick clump of bushes which grew beside the path, and stripped it of its leaves.

"Here, marster, whip me," he said, pushing it into his hand, and pulling off his coat.

The Major gave him an impatient cut with the switch, as he might have given his shying horse, and flung it away.

"Do you suppose I want to be soiling my hands whipping a worthless rascal? What I want to know is, what made you run away? You are free enough at home, Heaven knows; lazy enough, anyhow; it breaks me to keep you worthless rascals."

He paused and waited, with his eye on the darkey, as if expecting a reply.

"What was it? sheer worthlessness?"

"Nor, suh, 't wa' n't. Dat man say he was gwine meck you sell me," said Dick, doubtfully.

"Make me sell you? What man?"

"Dat po' white man—Mist' Bailiff." The negro's sovereign contempt was in his tone.

"Don't you let me hear you speak of my overseer that way, sir," said the Major; but he did not look offended. Perhaps he was secretly a little pleased. The negro recognized him as his natural and rightful chief, and looked on the other with unfeigned disdain.

"Make me sell you?" he repeated. "Who ever made me do anything? If he could have made me sell you, I 'd have sold you long ago, for you are not worth keeping. Come along home with me this minute." He rode on, the negro following.

The latter was walking behind, and could have easily enough slipped off into the woods and have escaped; but he did not attempt it. His master's will controlled him, as an officer controls a soldier in battle. Indeed, as he followed him, his whole manner had changed. The look of doubt and difficulty had disappeared from his face, and he even grinned to himself every now and then.

When they had crossed the river to their own side, and come in sight of the fields through the woods, the Major stopped.

"You 'd better go back by yourself," he said; "it will be better for you. If you come with me, they will think I brought you back. Go that way." He pointed through the woods in a direction at right angles to the road they were in.

The negro hesitated, and made a gesture of embarrassment.

"Marster—"

"If the overseer says anything to you, tell him I told you to say he was to come to see me." The Major thought that was his doubt.

"Nor, suh, 't ain' dat," explained the darkey. "Dat feller Pokeberry,—Pokeberry Green, dat nigger-hunter—" He paused.

"Well, what about him?" demanded the Major.

"He 's a bad feller!" he said earnestly.

"I thought he had dogs?" the Major said dryly, with a quizzical look in his eyes.

The negro missed the point.

"He got meanness in him!" he said. "He got he mine set for you and Marse Bruce, too; and for dem folks over yonder, too." He indicated Dr. Browne's place, across the river. "He got meanness in him!"

"Here, how do you know this?" the Major demanded.

The negro paused.

"I heah him say so. I been up to he house."

"Been up to his house?"

"Yes, suh; I crope up dyah t'other night, and hearn him tellin' another man all about hit."

"I though he had dogs," said the Major.

"Dem ar little houn's!" said the negro, dis-

214

dainfully. ''I don' mind dem no mo' 'n I does mices. I done meck friends wid 'em,'' he said, with a shrewd gleam in his eyes.

The Major looked amused.

''Well?''

''I hearn him say,'' the negro proceeded, ''dat he was gwine long back whar he come f'om; dat he was tired o' livin' down heah; he could go back dyah now, he said, 'cus ev'ybody is done dead whar knowed him. But b'fo' he go, he said, he was gwine 'lef he mark behind him,' and he name dem he gwine lef he mark on.''

The fellow's seriousness testified his truth, and the Major listened attentively.

''He say he gwine lef he mark on you, marster, and Marse Bruce, an' on dat ole man'' (again indicating the direction beyond the stream), ''and de young lady over dyah. He said he could ketch her, and sometimes when she was out in de woods he was gwine fine her; an' Marse Bruce, he said he 'd git him ef he hang for it. Dat man 's got meanness in him!'' he said again.

''You heard him say all this?'' said the Major, thoughtfully.

''Yes, suh; an' a heap mo', too. I been know him some time.'' He gave a quick glance at his master. "I been know him ever since dat time he cotch me and fotch me back tied, an' you 'buse him so." (The Major looked virtuous.) "He never forgive you for dat," proceeded the negro. "He meet me once, an' ax me did n' warn' run away for good. He say whar he come f'om de niggers was all free, and had big house and mule like white folks, and ef I 'd come wid him, he could git me dyah; dat we could slip off some night, and go like I b'longst to him, tell we git whar he live, or somewhar or nother."

"Ah! Well, and—what?"

"I tell him, Nor, I run away enough now. I don' warn be no free-nigger. I know I ain' gwine meck out I b'longst to him," he said, with contempt; "not to dat mean, po' white man." He thought of the time he had caught and tied him, and of the other occasion when he had had him whipped; but did not deem it worth while to recall these to his master. "An' it good I did n'; cause dat night I talkin' 'bout, I heah him tellin' dat turr man I ain' know, 'bout how he had try to git me to go off wid him, an' ef he had, he wuz gwine teck me down to South Cyarliny an' sell me. He say he done sole two or three down dyah in he time, an' he laughed and tried to git de urr man to go in wid him. Dat man got meanness in him!"

The Major was thoroughly attentive.

"Was that all you heard him say?"

"Yes, suh, den," said the negro. "I got skeered de dogs mought git to barkin', an' meck him let he gun off an' put he mark on me, an' I slipped off. He over yonder in de woods now." He nodded over towards the other side of the stream. "I don't know ef he arter Marse Bruce or dat young lady."

"Go home," said the master, "and don't say anything of this to any one."

"Yes, suh."

He went off, and the Major rode on.

On the way through the fields he met his overseer, who, unfortunately for him, recurred to the conversation of the morning. The Major broke out on him:

"Sell one of my negroes? No, sir! I'd as soon think of selling you. I don't care how often the fellow runs away. He must have had some cause I don't know about. I'd have run away, too."

This was a deadly thrust at the overseer, who looked dumbfounded, and with much humility said something about the Major's speech this morning.

"Well, sir, I never had the least intention of it," he said truly. "I thought you knew me well enough by this time to be able to tell when I mean a thing and when I do not."

He rode on to the house. As he entered the hall his eyes fell on the portrait of his grandmother as a bride, which hung on the wall.

"By Jove! how like her she is!" he said. "She looks as proud as she was, and she was the proudest woman on earth."

At that moment Margaret Reid, her pride forgot, was seated on the low porch with her head on her arm, where she had flung herself more than an hour before. The basket of wild flowers she had gathered was overturned on the floor beside her, and the flowers lay wilting in the sun.

XVII

WHEN the Major arrived at home, the first thing he did was to consult his wife. This he always did whatever the matter might be, though he did not invariably follow her advice, —an independence he atoned for by being always ready to admit its folly.

As he came out the audience chamber, his wife called after him:

"Let Dick drive them over."

The Major gave her a look of admiration as he passed out of the door.

A half-hour later Dick Runaway was driving out of the gate of the river pasture the two finest milch cows in the Major's herd. The Major rode down, and joining him, accompanied him to the other side of the river to see the cows safely across. As he turned back he called to the negro:

"Be sure to remember, you are not to mention who sent them."

This Dick faithfully engaged not to do; and the Major rode slowly home as he saw him start the cows up the hill, along the old road through the pines.

Just as he emerged from the woods he was met by Bailiff, his overseer, in a state of great excitement. A negro had found him on some other portion of the plantation, and told him that a man had been seen down in the river pasture actually driving two of the Major's cattle out of the field. He was thought to be Dick Runaway. He was following on their tracks in hot haste.

"You 'd better sell that nigger, sir," he said earnestly. "He 's ruinin' every one on this place."

The Major looked quite sheepish. He told the overseer with much embarrassment that he had himself directed Dick to drive the cows over to a neighbor's; that Mrs. Landon had heard his family was very poor, and wished to relieve them.

It was this same day, towards the afternoon. Old Dr. Browne was sitting alone in his room. He had made Margaret get him pen, ink, and paper, and then had sent her out to walk. She had found her mammy getting ready to go after the cows; and as the old woman was ailing with rheumatism, which she called "a misery in her back," had told her she would go in her place, and with an injunction to her to look after her grandfather, had gone off through the pines down towards the pond where the cows usually roamed, sustaining themselves on the coarse pond-grass.

She had not been gone long when the old woman coming to her door on the way to the house to fulfil Margaret's injunction, saw two cows being let into the yard at the old gate by a negro man.

With an exclamation of astonishment at the strange sight, she hastened to meet the man at as rapid a pace as her lameness permitted.

"Whose cows is dem you got dyah? and what you drivin' em thoo heah for? Don't you know marster don't 'low folks to be drivin' stock thoo dis place?"

She spoke with some asperity in her voice. It was a little tempered by the sight of the sleek coats and large, milky bags of the cows, at which she looked with the eye of a connoisseur.

"Good evenin'," said the man, who was Dick Runaway. "Dey 's Dr. Browne's cows."

"Dem ain' we cows," said the old woman.

"We ain't got but two cows, an' dee 's po'er 'n dem."

"I cyarn help it," said Dick; "dese is de doctor's."

"Don't I know my own cows? Often as I been milked Teensey and Princess!" She looked scornfully at him.

" 'Pears like you don't," said he, with an air of mystery about him; " 'cuz I tell you dese is Dr. Browne's cows."

"Whar he git 'em, den?" she asked, resting her doubled fists on her hips.

This was a question Dick was unprepared for. He remembered the Major's injunction that he was on no account to say a word as to who sent them.

"Whar he git 'em?" he asked vacantly, to gain time whilst he hunted around for a plausible lie. "Whar he git 'em? What you got to do wid whar he git 'em? I tell you he got 'em. Ain' dat 'nough for you to know? You better go 'long an' git bucket to milk 'em, cause milk running out de bags right now. You ain' never see no sich cows as dese befo'!" He could not help indulging in a little bragging, and was congratulating himself on his reply.

"I believe you 'se done stolt dem cows, and

jes' tryin' to lef 'em heah to git youself out o' trouble, an' git we in,'' said the old lady, suspiciously.

This completely disarranged Dick's plans and disposed of his complacency. He vowed, with many asseverations, that he had not only come by the cattle honestly, but had been instructed by his master to bring them as a present to Dr. Browne; and he was led into such a glowing description of his master's wealth and grandeur, that before he was half through, the old woman had learned fully all the facts in the case.

She asked if he had brought a note. Dick, thoroughly humbled, said he had not. So with a sniff at him and his master she accepted the cows without the note, and made Dick drive them down to the ''back yard.''

There she dismissed him, with a message of thanks, couched in such language and accompanied by an air of so much condescension, that Dick left with a mystified feeling, partly astonishment, and partly awe.

''Dat ain' no po' white folks' nigger,'' he said to himself again and again, as he went home. ''She talk jes' as assumptious as ef she b'longst to marster.''

When the old woman had seen Dick well out

of sight her whole manner changed. In place of the indifference she had displayed before him, delight beamed from her wrinkled black face, and importance showed in every movement she made.

After she had first secured and made friends with the two cows, and milked them a little to satisfy herself, she went into the house to acquaint her master with the important news. Her eager manner, however, was put off, like a garment, at his door, and when she entered his chamber she was as quiet, and apparently as calm, as usual.

The old gentleman was lying back in his chair, with his eyes closed. His pen was in his hand and his paper was on his knee. She thought he was asleep, and was retiring, when he spoke her name.

"Clarissa?"

"Sir?"

"Come here."

She obeyed, and stood silent near his chair. "Where is your mistress?" he asked.

"She gone arter de cows. She would go, suh; I could n' hender her."

He closed his eyes again and kept them shut. She remained motionless.

"That young man,—ah—young Mr. Landon, over the other side of the river,—ah—you have seen him over on this side?"

"Yes, suh."

"Ah! How often?" He put the questions very slowly, and as if they fell between his thoughts.

"I ain' never seen him but once, suh, not to speak to," she said; "but he comes over heah right constant. He 'pears to be mighty fon' o' fishing over heah, though I don' think he ketches much."

"What sort of a young man—ah—what does he seem to be doing when he is n't catching fish?"

"He 'pears to me, marster, to be kind o' trompin' up an' down. He ain' arter fish, marster; he 's arter my mistis, my lamb," she broke out suddenly.

Her master made no reply, but he opened his eyes and looked at her without moving. Her tongue being loosed, she went on to tell him all she knew of Bruce, who she declared appeared to her to be "a mighty nice disposed gent'man." She instanced his going to drive the cows back the day they went across the river.

"I know—I know," said her master, when

225

she paused after her account. "I am getting very old and feeble, I think I shall write a will. I had not intended to do so, but I think now I shall. I wish you to know where it is if anything should happen."

"Yes, suh."

Then she proceeded to tell of the present of the two cows, which she attributed to Bruce.

This piece of news had a very different effect on the old gentleman from that which she expected. It threw him into a violent passion. He declared that he would not submit to such insolence, and directed that the cows should be forthwith driven home. He would write a note. No; no note had been sent with them; none should go back with them, but a message to Major Landon to say that he had cows of his own, and "wanted neither his cows nor his damned patronizing interference."

Old Clarissa was aghast. She could not understand her master's wrath over what she considered a sort of miraculous generosity which had come just in the nick of time; but she felt that her master must have some good reason for his position and she bowed before it.

The cows accordingly reappeared that evening at the Landon Hall barn, with a message which had lost none of its vigor by transmission through either old Polium or the overseer to whom he delivered it. To be repulsed in the moment when we are flattering our souls that we have been generous is hard to forgive. In fact, the Major felt that he had taken a liberty with his strange neighbor, and he recognized that he had gotten soundly snubbed for it. After receiving the message the Major burnt at white heat; even Mrs. Landon's soothing influence having no effect on him.

When, after having started the cows home in her husband's charge, the old woman returned to her master, as he instructed her to do, he was just folding up the paper which he had written. He made her light a candle and bring a piece of sealing-wax, and with it he sealed the document carefully, using a large seal containing a crest, which he had on his watch chain. Then he endorsed it with the words:

"Statement and Will of him known as Thomas Browne, M. D., of Landon Hill. Written wholly with his own Hand. To be opened only after his Death."

This paper he gave to the old woman and directed her where to place it in a drawer in an old desk in the corner, explaining to her with great care what it was, and impressing on her its importance in event of his death at any time. She promised, with an earnestness which satisfied him, that it should be preserved and produced, and with a wave of his hand he dismissed her.

As she disappeared, he sank back on his pillow, and his eyes closed.

"It was her due," he said to himself wearily. "I had not intended it; but it was her due. I have sacrificed everything, even her, to what I deemed my expiation, and, perhaps, after all it was but my pride. It has been my curse all my life. I will not sacrifice her further. It shall not pursue her after my death. I will make the amend to her. I will humble them. 'Humble them!' " he repeated. "There it is again! God forgive me! it comes up even in my best action. It has ruined my life! blasted all it has touched! made me an outcast! left her a beggar!"

He leaned back with an expression of unutterable weariness on his gray face. In his eyes was something of the look of an imprisoned eagle.

XVIII

MARGARET was looking for the cows down in the old pine-grown field on the river. She had wanted the walk; wanted anything that would take her out of herself. Her face, her every motion showed that she was undergoing a struggle. As she passed along the paths now in shade, now in sunshine, her form straight, her step swift and easy, her brow now puckered, now clearing, her supple limbs just outlined by her summer dress, she might have been a young Diana pondering her revenge for some too bold hunter who had invaded her domain.

The time that had passed since her interview with Major Landon had been new to her; her life had been different. Why had he come to see her? Did Bruce Landon love her? He had never himself intimated it. And had she not promised that she would not marry him? Given her word, which shut him out from her forever! Would she—could she marry him against the will of that hard, cruel father of his, with his thin, proud face and his cold words? How dared he to speak so to her! How dared he come to her at all! It was an insult. She, poor as she was, would humble his pride. Her grandfather was better than he. Had not her mammy told her of his heroism when the whole country was stricken with fever and when even the closest ties of blood were relaxed; when the people looked to him almost as to a saviour! It was he who had buried the dead, cared for the suffering and inspired courage in the living. He had been like a guardian angel to a whole city. And how dared that man come to her as he had done! She would show him that she, too, was proud. And even as she walked along the well-known paths through the pines, she at the thought held her head more erect and stepped with a more offended mien. But there it came again: the picture of the handsome, calm, white face upturned, with the eyes closed and the lashes on his cheek, just as he had lain on the floor at her feet that evening when she thought he was dead, murdered by that ruffian. Why could she not forget it? Why had her heart stopped beating, and then leaped into her throat? She had thought of him as he lay that afternoon so long ago, asleep on his arm under the great poplar with

230

the sunbeams on his beautiful, upturned face, as she had kissed him for the fairy prince to bring him to life. Why had she longed so to throw herself beside him as he lay that night on the floor, and die with him? Why had she thought of him all these years? Why had she ever seen him? Was he not infinitely beyond her? Besides, had she not promised not to marry him, never to marry him?

She clenched her slender hands as she walked along, and pressed the nails into her pink palms till they hurt.

She could see or hear nothing of the cows along the branch where they could usually be found, so she went on towards the river, thinking they might be there. She had walked that path a thousand times, yet she now thought only of the occasions when she had met Bruce Landon. She would never see him again; for his cruel, hard father would tell him what she had said. He would be angry with her for refusing to marry him when he had never even said a word to her. She pictured to herself his indignation when his father should inform him of her promise. What right had she to assume that he wanted to marry her? She did not know even that he loved her. He would go away and stay

231

another eight years; he would never come back. She would not marry him if he did.

She stopped to listen, trying to think it was for the cow-bells; but the sorrowful notes of a dove's "Coo-coo-oo, Coo-oo-oo" on some dead limb deep in the pines were the only sound she heard, and they made the silence and loneliness more oppressive.

She turned and went towards the big spring at the foot of the great poplar.

Was it to find the cows?

She had almost reached the spring, when, at a turn in the path, she came face to face with a man.

Her heart leaped into her throat with fear; for she recognized at once the burly figure, the coarse, bloated face crossed by the deep red mark which had given his name to Pokeberry Green. He had in his hand his gun. He broke into a coarse laugh as he observed the start she gave.

"So you were lookin' fer me, my pretty lady," he said with a leer, resting his gun on the ground, and standing in the middle of the narrow path. "I 'm havin' luck to-day."

"Good evening; I was looking for my cows," said Margaret in as calm a voice as she could

232

command, moving out of the path to let him pass.

"Lookin' fer the cows; en' warn' you lookin' fer nothin' else? Well, now, maybe I 'll help you look fer 'em. Pleasant to find comp'ny in a lonesome place onexpected, ain' it? Kind o' lonesome place down here on the river?" The fellow laughed amusedly at the girl's frightened look.

"Let me pass, please," she said coldly, moving to go by him.

"Oh, don' be in sich a hurry," he drawled. "We ain' met in a long time,—not to talk, though I 've seen you often. I wuz lookin' fer somebody, something else besides you, an' not ixpectin' to fine sich pretty game, sich a pretty little duck, and I cain' bear to give you up. Don' frown that way; 't ain' becomin' to sich a pretty face. Cain' you smile a little on Poke?"

"Let me by, sir; don't you dare to speak to me!" said Margaret, raising her head defiantly and looking at the ruffian with flashing eyes.

He was somewhat abashed, and changed his drawling tone; but as she moved, he seized her by the wrist.

"You vixen!" he growled; "I 've got you now; I have been waiting fer you."

Margaret was naturally wiry, and fear and anger together gave her unwonted strength. With a cry of anguish and fright, she wrenched her arm from his grasp, lacerating the wrist, and springing forward fled like a frightened deer down the path.

"Ah! That's your game?" laughed the ruffian, running after her. "You are worth catching. Stop, or I'll shoot."

Margaret fled the faster.

He was overtaking her when he suddenly stopped, and turned his head, and listened; for a shout was heard down the path a short distance ahead, and the sound of a man's footsteps rushing towards them. Pokeberry sprang into the bushes and dashed away, just as Margaret rushed into the arms of Bruce Landon.

"Oh, Bruce, Bruce!" she cried.

The next instant she was weeping hysterically, and his strong arms were supporting her.

When the delirium had passed, Margaret found herself sitting on the great rock by the spring. Bruce was beside her, and his arm was around her. Then she remembered. She remembered how she had clung to him; how she had loved him; how safe she had felt in his arms, as if he alone could shield and save her; how he had soothed her, calmed her, comforted her; how furious he had been with the ruffian who had insulted her; and how he would have followed him and caught him, and, she believed, have killed him, but for her clinging to him, and telling him that she would die if he left her there; then how he had kissed her and told her of his love; and how, with her face against his, she had told him that she loved him; and how she could willingly have died there in his arms. All this she now, for the first time, remembered.

Her head was on his shoulder, and his arm was around her, and she rested with a sense of such perfect security and happiness that when the recollection of the promise to his father came suddenly to her it smote her like the shock of death. She could not act. She could not give him up. Stronger and stronger, however, came the recollection of her position and of the humiliation which Major Landon had placed on her, —on her and on her grandfather. She thought of the old gentleman sitting lonely in his armchair in the bare room at home. She thought of his patience, of his kindness, and of his pride. What a blow it would be to him to know it! She opened her eyes and gazed straight before her for a moment, thinking it all over.

Suddenly she sprang up with a movement so unexpected that Bruce started, and gazed about him, supposing some one was approaching.

Margaret looked at him, her lips half formed for speech. An expression of deep anxiety had taken the place of the look of perfect content which had made her face so sweet.

"Well, what is it?" Bruce reached out his hand to her, with a smile, and then rose to take her again in his arms.

"No; I cannot. I have been wrong. I cannot marry you, ever, and I have no right to love you; it is impossible. No." She backed away with a gesture of refusal, as Bruce caught her, and with the smile still on his lips, attempted to draw her to him and put his arm around her. Her face was perfectly grave, and the happiness was dying slowly from it as the light fades from an evening sky.

"What are you talking about?" he asked.

"Oh! I cannot. No," (as he tried to draw her to him), "no. Oh, why did I ever see you? Why did you ever come here?" She looked at him piteously, as if she asked the question to receive an answer. "Why did you ever come here?" she repeated.

"I came because I loved you; because you are my soul; because God drove me here. I would have found you in a desert had you been there," declared Bruce, vehemently, catching her, and drawing her firmly up to him. She put up her hands, and placing them on his shoulders, held him at arm's length.

"No; you must not. I cannot; indeed I cannot. I was wild, insane; it is impossible. I cannot love you." She kept him from her by an effort of strength.

"But you do love me; you said you did."

"No; I was wrong. You cannot love me."

"But I can, and I do,—better than earth, better than heaven," declared Bruce, catching and holding her by her arms.

"No; you have no right to do it. I am nothing but an unknown, poor girl. I know nothing; I have seen nothing. You are Bruce Landon. Your father—"

He would have interrupted her, but she would not permit him.

"—hates me. Your mother—"

"My mother is an angel," declared the young man, rejoiced to find one point he could combat.

Her eyes softened, and she wavered.

"Is she? What is she like?"

Bruce seized the opportunity.

"She is an angel," he repeated earnestly. "She is as beautiful in character and mind as she is in person, and she is the most beautiful woman in the world. One of the two most beautiful," he added, his admiration showing in his eyes. "My mother would adore you, and you her," he said.

She sighed. But the thought of her grandfather came back to her; of him sitting alone in his room. Then the thought of Major Landon came, as he had sat on his handsome horse, looking over her head, and asking her to "take a message to the young woman there, Dr. Browne's grand-daughter—Miss Browne, or whatever her name was." A hot wave of shame swept over her. It was an insult.

With an effort she suddenly released herself from Bruce's grasp.

"It is impossible," she said in a changed voice. "I can never marry you."

"But I don't understand?" broke in Bruce. "You have told me that you love me."

"No; I was wrong; I do not. I cannot. Your father—I will not marry you."

"My father has nothing to do with me," declared Bruce. "I love you. I have loved you all my life—ever since you were a little girl, and I waked and found you at my side." He caught her hand and held it fast.

"You should obey your father," she said.

"I will not obey him—not where you are concerned. I would not weigh the world against you." His passion drove her from her position.

"You have never been to see my grandfather. I will never marry—I will never love any one without his approval—his full approval," she said, faltering, her resolution waning.

"But I will get it," he said eagerly. "I asked you to let me go and see him, and you would not; you remember?"

"Yes; but you should have gone, anyhow," she said weakly, driven from her position.

"I will go now. Come."

He started to turn, drawing her with him. His face was eager with determination.

"No; you are so hasty," she said, weakening before his decision.

"Ah! you are just teasing me!" exclaimed Bruce. He caught her, and, breaking down the barrier of her arms, kissed her almost violently.

She remained quiet in his arms a moment, and then tried to free herself again.

"You must listen. You must not kiss me. I will not love you."

"I will kiss you. I will not listen. You shall love me!" He kissed her again.

"I am not teasing you," she said gravely, as he smiled down into her eyes. "You must go away, and not come here any more."

"I will not go away. I tell you now, I will not," said Bruce. "You have given yourself to me; you have opened the gates of heaven to me, and you shall not shut them; no one shall." He kissed her again. "You love me, don't you? Tell me." His eyes were searching hers.

"Yes; I do." Her eyes met his bravely.

"Then you will marry me?"

"No; I cannot. I will not. I have promised—" She stopped.

"Promised whom?" A sudden pang of jealousy shot through him.

"I cannot tell."

"You shall; you must." He seized her, and looked into her eyes. "You must tell me."

She was unable to resist him. His face was so close to hers, his eager gaze fascinated her. His will dominated her will. She felt that his word was a command which she could not disobey.

"Tell me," he repeated quietly; "whom have you promised?"

"Your father." She looked him in the eyes, and spoke the words in a low voice, almost timidly.

"My father! When did you see him?"

"Yesterday; he came yesterday, and I promised him." She looked at him humbly, almost fearfully.

"Well; you shall unpromise him. He shall release you," he said, after a pause, quietly, but with absolute confidence as he released her hand and straightening himself stood before her, his face calm and touched with a new loftiness; and, for the first time, she looked down. And she let him put his arm around her, and draw her to him; and quietly laid her head on his shoulder. She felt that he had taken charge of the matter, and lifted the responsibility from her. She felt that he had taken her life into his charge and protection. And once more the sound of a dove cooing for its mate came from deep down in the woods, a note of Peace.

XIX

WHEN Bruce left her in the summer evening light he had obtained from her a promise that she would meet him at the spring the following evening at sunset. His father was absent from home, but was to return in the morning, when he would extort from him a full release, and absolute permission for him to claim the fulfilment of her promise. He knew there would be a struggle and possibly a serious breach; but he was prepared to face all consequences and he had no doubt that he would secure what he demanded, and she had suddenly learned to take her views from him. She wondered how she could ever have doubted him. He had won her. She imposed these two conditions, that he should bring his father's release from her pledge, and win her grandfather's consent. He walked with her to the top of the hill, and then bade her good-by. He went over, word by word, all he had told her of his love. He would die for her.

When he left her, the last glimpse she had of

him was as he turned again to kiss his hand to her: a radiant picture of a gallant young lover for whom the world held only one thing: his love.

"I love you," she heard him call. He was clearly outlined against a bit of blue evening sky in a break of the trees, tall and straight, and as she looked back at him she felt that he was her master. The walk home was full of joy for him the earth was no longer the same he had known that morning. He trod on air. Heaven was about him. Even the thought of his father's disappointment and disapproval could not damp his ardour. He must give way to him. He must participate in his joy. Why, since he had seen Margaret, he could not fail to admire her, to love her.

Such is love's way. It changes everything in its alembic and leaves only love.

When Bruce arrived at home, he found, as he expected, that his father was not there. The Major had gone to the court-house, some twenty-five miles away, to appear before the grand jury. He had determined to have the jury present Pokeberry, and, perhaps, the other rioters who had attacked Dr. Browne's house. Not that the old creature ought not to be driven out, he explained, but that was not the way to do it. Perhaps, he might present him, too. But he would not have a gang of drunken blackguards trespassing on private property, and attacking a man in his own house. It was an outrage on the Commonwealth. Besides, he would no longer submit to such a scoundrel as Pokeberry going unwhipped of justice.

After all, deep down in his heart was the fear that the ruffian might do Bruce an injury. He knew how, even from Bruce's boyhood, there had been a mortal hatred between them; and, of course, since Bruce had foiled him in his attack on Dr. Browne, the ruffian had a new grudge against him, and the boy was always going where the scoundrel might easily waylay him. If anything should happen to Bruce, what should he do? The thought made him tremble. Under all his sternness, he loved his son passionately. He was his pride, his idol.

He did not return until the following afternoon. He was in high good humor.

Just after his arrival, Bruce found him in the library. He greeted him pleasantly.

"Come in. Well, sir, I have at last set the law in motion, and I think we shall be rid of that ruffian Pokeberry for a little while at least," he began. "Hall will have him by to-morrow night unless he skips the country."

Bruce, however, was too impatient to delay longer the subject which engrossed his thoughts. He merely acknowledged the speech with a bow, and at once demanded a release of the promise the old gentleman had obtained from Miss Reid. In a moment there was an explosion. The serenity in which the Major returned after having accomplished his purpose at the court-house gave way to a passion of anger, and he raged over Bruce's revolt.

He positively refused. The young man, however, sobered by his love for Margaret, or by the gravity of the step he was taking, remained cool, and firmly demanded the release.

"May I ask, sir, what you propose to support this young woman on?" inquired the Major, with an exasperating manner.

"Indeed, sir, I have not considered that matter," replied Bruce, disdainfully. "It is one which I think only concerns her and me."

"It concerns you rather closely. I think you had better consider it. You are not counting, I hope, on my generosity."

"I never count on your generosity," replied the young man, with a serenity which stung the

Major. "I might count on your charity; but never on your generosity."

"You are presuming on my charity now," said the Major, sternly.

"When I found that you had taken the trouble to go, before I had even declared my love for the young lady," said Bruce, "and had exacted a promise from her to reject my addresses when they should be made, I could do no less than arrange to have her released, so that at least she might be free to act; and I thought it would be indelicate to discuss any other matters. As you secured from her a rejection of me when I was the prospective heir to your opulence, I hardly imagine the loss of that honor will add greatly to the danger of my refusal."

"Bruce," said the Major, making an effort to remain cool, "consider carefully what you are doing. If you marry that young woman—" He paused under the stress of his feelings. "If you but ask her to marry you—" He paused again, unwilling to complete the threat; for Bruce straightened himself, and looked him full in the eyes.

"I have asked her to marry me," he said; "I love her, and I will marry her against both heaven and hell."

He suddenly broke out, and passionately demanded a release of the promise she had given.

The Major rose from his chair.

"Take it, and convey it to her with my compliments," he said, standing straight and white, waving his hand to the door. "And marry her, and sink down to her level, a shame and disgrace to your name. Leave the house, and, after you marry that woman, never come into my presence again."

Bruce's breast heaved. His face was deadly white, and his hands were clenched.

"No other man on God's earth should speak to me so and live. I accept your release and your condition," he said almost quietly, looking his father fearlessly in the face. Then he turned and went out.

It was late when Bruce reached the old spring where he was to meet Margaret. The deep quietude of the summer afternoon filled the woods. Bruce dropped down at the foot of the old poplar, and leaned back against it as he had done so often before. He was waiting for Margaret—his Margaret.

A deep happiness filled his breast, driving out all thought of the stormy scene with his father. The pain it caused him had passed

247

away. Perhaps, his mother could help him; at least, she would never forsake him. However thoughts of them might recur hereafter, there was no place for them in his heart now. His memory was too full of Margaret—Margaret who belonged to him—Margaret who was his life. As he half sat, half inclined, on the ground, with the back of his head against the tree-trunk, he thought of the first time he had ever seen her. It was on that very spot. He had opened his eyes, and she had sat by his side. There was the sky he remembered as he dropped off to sleep; there were the same soft sounds, the woodwren in the alders below, the call of the ploughmen across the pond to their teams; the same cow-bells brokenly chiming far up the pond. It made him drowsy, and he let his eyes close, and thought of Margaret. He dreamed he heard Margaret coming nearer, nearer, and then—!

XX

ALL day Margaret had gone about as in a
dream. She seemed to have found a new
world.

The sun was almost down when she slipped
softly out of her room, and, gliding across the
little space in the rear of the house, which was
still kept clear for a yard, entered the wood by
the old path which led down to the spring. The
sun's rays came slanting through the trees. It
was later than she had supposed. She had not
intended to be so late, but the time had slipped
away. She had wanted to look—to look right,
and it had taken longer than she had thought.
The old dresses were hard to choose between,
and then it took so long to fix exactly, the one
she selected; the little glass was so small. And
now suppose any one should see her? Mammy
would not matter; but if her grandfather should
hear her and call? At last, however, she was
safe within the screen of the encircling woods.

Had any one seen her as she passed, tripping

down along the shady path, he would indeed have been astonished. The dress that she had selected was an old lawn,—an empire dress,— as soft as feathers, and as light, faded by age to a tint which left the rosesprays just visible like shadows of roses which had once lain on the delicate white. The waist was short, and the skirt loosely flowing, showing the little high-heeled slippers, and a hint of the dainty ankle. The white throat and shapely neck showed above the low collar. It was the dress she had worn that night when he was wounded. What would he think of her? She felt that she knew.

She was startled, as she came in sight of the spring, to see a man disappear in the bushes. She was sure it was that Pokeberry Green. She stopped, but at the same moment she caught sight of Bruce lying on the other side of the tree, and instantly all her fear disappeared. His presence filled every place with safety. The man had evidently seen him, and had run away. She stood still and waited, to give whoever it was time to get well out of hearing before going further. Then she tripped on.

Bruce did not stir. Ah! he was asleep.

She would trip up and catch him, and surprise him. She remembered that time so long ago when she had found him lying there. She had kissed him then. A blush came to her cheeks in the evening light as she remembered it. She would not now. She would just catch him by putting her hands over his eyes. She tripped up softly, keeping the tree between them, and kneeling down, put her hands around and over his face.

Why, it was wet; he was crying!

She looked.

Good God! he was covered with blood! He was dead!

She sprang to her feet with a shriek which reached the ploughmen turning their slow mules at the end of the furrows the other side of the pond, and made them stop and listen, and which fell on the ears of the heavy man with the ugly scar on his neck, hurrying off through the pines with muttered oaths, and made him quicken his pace to a run.

In a flash she had taken it in. Pokeberry, that man she had seen, had murdered him. But he could not be dead. She laid his head gently down. She knew this was the way to do when one fainted. She felt his wrist; tore open his collar; felt his heart; ran to the spring, and dipping her handkerchief in, ran back and bathed his white face, washing the clotted blood from it, and from his hair. There was the place, a great, ugly gash on the head, over the eyes, as if he had been struck with a club or a hammer.

"Bruce! Bruce!" she called him.

No, he was dead.

She sat down and took his head in her lap. She was calm now, as calm as he was, and he was calm forever. He was hers now. She bent over and kissed him, thinking quite calmly of the first time she had kissed him when he lay there. She almost expected him to wake now as he had done then. Anyhow, he was hers. The blood still flowed a little. She tore a strip from her dress and bound up his head and stopped the flow. Then she stood up. What should she do? Her grandfather and Uncle Polium were both crippled and unable to walk, and mammy was away; gone after the cows.

The nearest place at which she could get help, —was—yes, she must go there. He had, she knew, crossed in a boat. She could carry him, she felt so strong; but that might start the bleeding again, and he might not be dead,—please God! he might not. Her hopes revived. She felt his pulse, his heart again, and then she dashed off.

ON NEWFOUND RIVER

It was not quite dusk in the great hall at Landon Hall. The Major was striding up and down, justifying himself to his wife for his treatment of Bruce. He had, in his anger and wounded pride, said hard things about him, and Mrs. Landon had been weeping. He still felt bitter towards him, but not so bitter as he had felt at first. He was, however, still saying hard things about him, for his pride was sorely wounded. Bruce had beaten him, had defied him, foiled him, overpowered him. No, he did not care, and he said so, his anger again rising against him.

"No; I don't care if he never enters that door again; he shall never enter it with her," he was saying, when there was a sound outside: a sound of hurrying steps; some one ran up the gravel walk, sprang across the veranda, and seizing the knob, turned it hastily, first the wrong way and then the right; the great door flew open, and an apparition faced him.

A young girl in a light dress dabbled with blood, her hair dishevelled, her face deadly white, her eyes wild, her hands outstretched covered with blood, stood before him.

Mrs. Landon gave a cry.

"In the name of God! what is it?" exclaimed the Major.

"He is dead! Murdered!" she gasped.

"Where? How? Who?"

"Bruce,—your son,—murdered at the spring! Dead!"

She swayed, as if about to fall.

"Good God!" The Major caught her and held her in his arms.

"Brandy!" he called; "brandy, quick!" It was brought by Mrs. Landon, and he poured some down Margaret's throat and revived her. She staggered to her feet. "Come, quick, for God's sake! It may not be too late. Come!" She pulled him to the door.

It was quite dark when they reached him. He was still lying as Margaret had left him, outstretched, motionless, unconscious. They carried him to the old doctor's, as the nearest place, and because Margaret ordered it. She had taken charge. Her grandfather might save him, she said. Once more she had become calm.

He was borne in and laid in her room, on her bed, where he had lain that night after he was wounded.

She had run forward and warned her grandfather, and when the men arrived, they met them, and she led them in in the dark. A candle was brought.

The old surgeon leaned over the body and began his examination.

"Brandy," he said. Some one handed it to him, and he poured a little between his lips.

"He is living," he murmured.

Margaret sank down on the floor in a heap.

They picked her up, and in a little while she revived and went out of the room.

A short time afterwards there was a knock at the outer door.

It was Mrs. Landon, who had come over on horseback, around the head of the pond. The Major went to meet her. She came in, her face deadly white, and fell on her knees silently beside the bed. She looked at no one; but, pressing her face against her son's arm, uttered a low moaning sound.

"There is no fracture," said the old surgeon, gently.

She made no answer. She only moved slightly and placed her hand on Bruce's hair.

The doctor uttered another sentence or two of encouragement, and went out to get some article. In a little while Margaret brought it in. Major Landon had meantime stepped out of the room, and Mrs. Landon was alone with her son. She was still on her knees beside him, but she

255

rose as Margaret entered. Margaret set the glass down and turned to leave. As she did so she glanced up. Mrs. Landon was looking at her, and their eyes met. The girl's eyes fell, and she stood still with her head bowed humbly.

"I know all," said Mrs. Landon, gently.

At the sound of her low voice Margaret caught her hand, and, raising it, kissed it. It was an act of obeisance to his mother. She looked up, and in an instant the two women were in each other's arms.

It was an hour afterwards when the old Doctor left Bruce's side again and went to his own room. Margaret followed him. A moment later the door opened, and the Major entered without warning.

The old man turned to him. It was the first time he had faced him. He was dressed in an old wrapper, and wore a black skull-cap, from under which his long white hair fell down to his shoulders. He raised his head as the Major entered, and gave him an almost fierce look from his piercing eyes.

"In God's name who are you?" demanded the Major.

The old man half turned away.

"What is that to you?" he said, in his deep

voice. "Have I ever wronged you? ever interfered with you? ever asked of you a favor? ever demanded of you a right? Let me alone. Go back to your son. He will get well. Take him home when he is well enough, and keep him there." He turned his back.

"No," said the Major, who had never taken his eyes from his face. "By —! you shall tell me who you are." He caught him by the arm almost fiercely, and turned him to the light.

"What is your name?"

"I have no name; my name is dead," said the old surgeon, with emotion. He moved away, then suddenly turned back and, catching Margaret who, with wide eyes was standing near him, her burning gaze on his face, he pulled her forward.

"I have no name; I am no one; but this child has a name and blood as good as yours, Major Landon. She is Charles Landon's great-granddaughter." He put her half before him.

"Good God!" exclaimed the Major.

He sprang forward and took the old surgeon in his arms. He embraced him almost fiercely again and again.

"Brother!" he said, with deep emotion. "My brother, my dear brother, my own brother!"

257

His voice sounded like a caress. He released him and caught him again, saying,

"My dear, dear brother!"

Both men were weeping. The old Doctor was completely overcome. His head sank, and his sobs were audible. Presently the Major let him go.

Margaret was standing by, deeply moved. She stepped to her grandfather's side.

"Oh, grandfather!" she said, putting her arms about him.

When she let him go, the Major turned to her with grave courtesy,—almost humility.

"I do not ask your pardon," he said. He took her hand, and, raising it, kissed it. It was an act of homage such as he had never before in all his life paid any other woman but his wife. "But I ask your leave to thank you for my son's life. I owe you everything. He and all I have are yours. I only ask that you will believe that I loved him better than all the world. He is wiser than I. I owe you his life."

Margaret flung herself into his arms and wept on his shoulder.

"I loved him so," she sobbed.

"He loved you also," he said, soothing her tenderly.

XXI

WHILST Bruce was lying thus unconscious between life and death, his would-be murderer was fleeing for his life. His attack on Bruce had put the neighborhood in a turmoil. Never had there been such excitement on Newfound. A hue and cry had been raised, and the whole district was out scouring the country for the murderer. Sam Mills took his old, long gun from the forks over his door, and without more than a word or two, but with an ugly glitter in his eyes, struck out for the woods. Squire Johnson, his old opposition and pomposity alike forgotten, had issued the warrant, and forthwith joined in the chase. Little Hall, forgetting his official formula about "the posse," enlisted the men, as he galloped from house to house, by simply calling to them "to git their guns and come on with me and Sam; Pokeberry 's done murdered that boy, Bruce Landon."

It was a sympathetic people, slow to catch; but when ignited, going up altogether like powder. The fire lighted had become a conflagration.

The whole country was out, and the general sentiment was that when the murderer should be caught, it would be useless to wait for a trial; a simple waste of time. Indeed, in every squad of men, one, at least, had a "plough-line" hanging on his arm, ready for use.

The neighborhood was scoured.

Yet, after twenty-four hours, no trace of him had been found. Many thought he had escaped and gone off "back up whar he come from." He had been saying, for some time, he was going to do so. The miserable cabin where he had lived was deserted, and the two little hounds were found inside; one dead on the floor, with its brains dashed out, the other, with an ugly gash in its head, where it had evidently been struck with the same intent. This was regarded as positive proof that Pokeberry had fled the country; and when the roads had been picketed and the woods scoured for twenty-four hours, many of the pursuers gave up and returned home. Little Hall, however, with the sheriffalty in his eye, and with a yet larger number, continued the search, though without success, and on the afternoon of the second day, he and a party were standing in the little yard in front of Poke-berry's cabin, discussing the futility of further search. Dick Runaway was among them, listen-ing anxiously. The little hound, which had es-caped Pokeberry's murderous hand, slid timidly out from under the house and became an object of interest.

"He might 'a' left them po' dawgs," said one, "seein' he made his livin' by 'em. They never done him no harm, anyways."

"It 's a d—d mean man as kills a dawg," de-clared Sam Mills.

"An' his own dawg, too."

"Any dawg," said Mills.

All assented to this proposition. Killing a dog was regarded as quite as unpardonable as murdering a man. The poor little beast, mean-time, with his tail between his legs, circled around the group and singled out the negro. He recognized in Dick an old friend, and almost wagged his tail at him. Dick stooped down and began to examine his wound, which became the general subject of discussion. This again aroused the feeling against Pokeberry, and re-sulted in a determination to make another effort to catch the murderer. A man who would treat his own dog that way was too dangerous to let escape.

The group went off again, leaving Hall, who was completely broken down, and another man to watch the house, in case Pokeberry should by any chance come back there. It was then about dusk.

Dick set out towards home, the maimed little hound following him. As he walked along, the negro appeared in deep thought. Every now and then he stopped and muttered to himself, and several times he stooped and petted the little animal at his heels, which dumbly responded. At last he stopped where a narrow path ran off at right angles to the one he was in.

"Done kill Marse Bruce, and mos' kill you, and warn sell me down to Souf Cyarliny," he muttered, as he stooped over the little creature. He stood up presently, and peered down the narrow path earnestly.

"Heah, come 'long," he said suddenly. "I boun' he down this way," and plunged down the path through the woods.

An hour later he was in the well-known territory of Landon Hill.

One seeing him threading the narrow cow-tracks would have supposed he was coon or 'possum hunting. The hound was in front, sniffing about, and several times started off. At last Dick took a stout cord, which was wrapped several times around his waist, and tied one end around the dog's neck, so as to control him. The waning moon rose late in the night, and let an uncertain and ghostly light fall through the trees.

All night long Dick remained in the woods, slowly threading path after path, penetrating the densest thickets on Newfound. The hound, now thoroughly interested, several times started off as if on a trail; but Dick pulled him up, and led him elsewhere.

"Dis ain' no 'possum hunt, you ole fool," he said, under his breath; "you know you ain' no 'possum dawg."

It was towards morning that, deep down in the pines on the bank of Newfound, the dog struck a trail which the negro let him follow. When he first came on it, his manner changed. Dick was about to draw him away; but the dog pulled so, that finally he let him go on. The trail went straight towards the river. At last, in a little patch of pale moonlight, Dick stooped and closely examined the ground.

A man's track, almost fresh, showed in the soft earth.

"Ah! heah he! de black, nigger-ketchin' devil!" he muttered.

Dick peered anxiously through the bushes. The dog, with his nose to the ground, pulled on the cord.

Dick paused.

"Dat man got meanness in him," he muttered to himself.

Suddenly he turned, and, pulling the dog after him, started back. He talked to the little beast reassuringly as he walked along. "I know whar he is now; you need n' be feared, we gwine ketch him. He ain' gwine nowhar b'fo' we git back. I jes' gwine for help. I knowed he was down dyah," he concluded triumphantly.

In a little while he was in sight of the little, mean-looking shanty where Pokeberry had lived. He reconnoitred the space before him and, stooping, approached cautiously; for he knew the two men were on watch, and they might mistake him for the occupant.

His precaution was, however, unnecessary; for, when he crept up to the door, both men were fast asleep on the floor.

Hall, who had been up all the night before, had

set the other man as his subordinate, on guard for the first watch, and had pulled off his heavy boots and gone regularly to sleep; and the guard had duly followed suit, with an easy conscience, after a short interval.

The negro stole up to the constable and touched him.

"Mr. Hall!"

There was no response. Then he shook him.

"Mr. Hall! Marse Jim!"

At the second or third shaking, Hall sprang up, and, still half asleep, seized his gun.

" 'T ain' nobody but me, Marse Jim,—Dick, —Major Landon's Dick," said the negro.

"Oh! I thought 't was that scoundrel Poke-berry," said the little officer, in a disappointed tone. "I dreamt he was comin' up the path."

"Nor, suh; but I done fine him," said the negro.

In a second the little constable was wide awake. He began to pull on his boots vigorously. His first impulse was to get a posse; but as he got on his boots, his courage increased. The glory of catching the murderer alone dawned on him. The sheriffalty—the goal of his highest ambition—suddenly loomed up in sight.

The sound slumber of his companion who, with his head on his arm, and his mouth wide open, slept peacefully on even through the noise of Hall's stamping in getting on his boots, remained unbroken.

"Come on; me an' you can ketch him," said the constable to the negro, picking up his gun. A loud snort from his friend caught his ear. He gave him a look of contempt.

"He 's a —— of a guard," he said; "ain' he! Pokeberry could have come and knocked both our brains out like he done that boy's. Come along."

He picked up a rope which lay on the floor, and gave it to the negro.

Dick was not afraid. He possessed plenty of physical courage. All he wanted was the leadership—the moral support of a white man. His face now looked eager enough, as, calling the little hound, the two men disappeared down the path in the pines.

It was just daybreak, when, deep down in the marsh, the dog suddenly stopped, and raising his head, gave a low growl, his tail dropping, and every hair on his thin back rising.

"Ah!" said the negro, under his breath, seizing him. "Don' you bark."

266

Hall cocked his gun.

They held a little whispered consultation, and then the negro crept forward, Hall following at his heels with his gun ready. Reaching a heavy clump of bushes, Dick parted them and peeped through. When he turned, his eyes were almost popping out of his head. He pointed silently for Hall to look.

Ten feet ahead, on the ground, under a tree, lay a heavy man fast asleep on his back. The breast of his coarse dirty shirt was open, and his thick red neck showed the deep purple mark of Pokeberry. An empty whiskey-flask was near him. A gun lay beside him, and the handle of an ugly knife peeped out from his belt. Another consultation was held, and then Dick, taking the rope, and making a large running knot, crept forward, whilst Hall brought his gun half up, ready for use if it were needed. Carefully placing the open large loop around one of the sleeper's hands, which was raised from the ground and enabled him to adjust it, Dick suddenly jerked it tight. The murderer, with an oath, sprang up into a sitting posture. As he did so, the negro gave a turn of his rope around his other hand, and then, with a dexterous twist, wrapped it around his neck, and pulled it taut.

Pokeberry lost a second trying to get at his knife, in which Dick gave another turn of the rope around his neck, and got his hands together. Pokeberry rose, but the negro flung himself on him. Even then it was a terrible struggle, and the clothes of the two men as they wrestled and rolled were torn to shreds.

Little Hall's gun was useless; for he could not shoot one without danger of shooting the other. He, however, jumped around and encouraged Dick with many oaths, standing ready to aid him if it should become necessary. It did not become necessary; for the liquor in Pokeberry's brain, and the tangle of cord around his wrists and neck decided the contest, and Dick finally had the murderer bound and subdued. His struggles but tightened the cords around his throat.

"Loosen this rope, for God's sake!" he gurgled. "I 'm chokin' to death." His eyes, in fact, looked as if he were speaking the truth.

"You 'member dat time you tied me, don't you? I got you now whar I want you. Wait till marster and them white mens gits hold of you," said Dick, "an' you 'll have a tighter rope 'n that roun' you' neck."

He, however, relieved the cord a little. This suggestion had its effect on the ruffian.

"What they goin' to do with me?" he asked. "Try me?"

"Hang you."

His jaws dropped. "When?"

"Dee got rope waitin' fer you now," said Dick.

The ruffian's red face turned deadly white.

"I did n't do it," he said. "I swear—"

"Yes, you did. Git up heah; I gwine carry you to him right now."

They lifted the fellow; but he dropped down again.

"Look here," he said; "if you all will let me get away, I 'll—I 'll give you anything in the world."

Hall laughed derisively.

"Get up, and come on."

"I would n' let you git 'way," said Dick, "not fer marster's big plantation an' ev'ry mule on it. Git up heah!"

The two men jerked at the rope till the brute, half strangled, agreed to come.

The twenty or more men assembled at the Crossroads that morning were a sleepy and dejected-looking set. Their search had failed; the

269

murderer had escaped. Little Hall's chance of the Sheriffalty, never very great, had vanished with him; and the coveted office would certainly go to the lower end of the County. Suddenly one of the group swore a great oath and pointed up the road. There came three men, the foremost with his hands and arms tied to his body, and behind him, Hall and Dick Runaway, walking like soldiers, with guns on their shoulders. A little hound trotted at Dick's heel. The crowd was instantly in a commotion. They streamed down the road to meet the captors and their prisoner.

Pokeberry was taken from the two, who were swept from their feet, and in a minute a rope was around his neck. He recognized his peril. His face was deadly white, and he began to plead. His pleading, however, was cut short. The mob was in no humor for mercy. He was dragged along to the Crossroads, where a brief stop was made, and was tied to a tree, whilst a consultation was held. It was determined to lynch him immediately. The crowd again surrounded him. One or two of them told him to pray. The poor wretch broke forth into cries. But the mob was pitiless. It contained a number who had been his boon companions. His many

270

offences were enumerated, the attack on Dr. Browne being one of them.

"Jim, you are the constable; you ought to protect me," he said to Hall.

"Protect you! I'm going to hang you," said Hall.

At this moment, a remark from Dick unexpectedly intervened and saved him.

The negro was most eager to have him die, but suggested that, maybe, his master would like to see him hanged. This opened a discussion; and by one of the freaks which frequently operate on a mob, it turned the scale, and it was decided to put the question to a vote, whether he should or should not be hanged till the Major could see him.

It was decided by a small majority that the hanging should be put off, as it could be at most for only a few hours.

The prisoner was locked up in a little outhouse on the premises, with guards over him. During the day, hundreds of people flocked to the place, and the little groggery did the largest business ever known, at least in whiskey. The guards furnished their part of the patronage, and exhibited the prisoner as if he had been a show.

271

By nightfall they were all in liquor, and were drinking heavily. Hospitality demanded that even a murderer should be treated properly in this respect, standing, as it were, somewhat in the room of a guest. Pokeberry had been furnished all the liquor he wanted. This was a great deal. He called for it frequently. At dark he was apparently drunk. His guards were certainly so.

The next morning, at daylight, the prisoner was gone. No one could tell how; and as there had been a heavy thunder-storm in the night, there was small chance of tracking him. The guards were too steeped in liquor and overwhelmed with confusion to give any coherent account. He had actually taken their guns with him. He had been there at two o'clock. One of them had taken a last drink with him. There was a great commotion. The guards were universally cursed and derided, and sought consolation in stupor.

A hue and cry was again raised, and the fugitive was hotly pursued. Dick Runaway and the little hound, whose reputations were established, were recognized as important factors in the chase, and were given honorable positions in the front.

The crowd struck for Newfound. The woods were systematically searched.

Toward sunset, the track of the fugitive was discovered. The hound had followed the scent to an old brush-pile, deep in a thicket. The fugitive had evidently lain there concealed. The brush was scattered about, as if he had left hastily. The little hound dashed off towards the water. He was making for the pond, and the dense thickets on the other side. The little beast, thoroughly interested, followed the trail with the precision of destiny. It cut straight for the river. It was evidently warm, for he gave mouth, his long, mellow note exciting the pursuers, who could scarcely keep up with him. Once the trail was lost for a little while, where the fugitive had waded in a branch; but the little animal picked it up again, and struck out confidently in the same direction.

At last, just at sunset, one of the pursuers caught sight of a figure on a knoll a few hundred yards ahead, running with all his speed. His shout gave new ardor to the chase, and the crowd, with loud cries, dashed through the bush to head him off from the pond.

It was, indeed, Pokeberry. All day he had lain concealed, crouched under a pile of brush in the pines, in a spot which he had found an hour or two after his escape. Newfound was up a little, and he could not cross safely just then; but it would fall by night, and he could get over.

He felt secure, and, overcome with fatigue and relief, had fallen asleep. How long he slept he could not tell.

He was aroused suddenly by shouts in the distance. He lay still. He was so concealed that they might pass within ten feet of him and miss him. But suddenly he started up, for the note of a hound, a note well known, reached his ears. A deep oath fell from his lips, and his face grew deadly white. It was his own dog, and he was on a warm trail; on his track? The notes came again clearer. They were nearer; they were on his trail. Springing up with an oath, and seizing his gun, he dashed through the woods. If he could get to the head of the pond, and reach the other side, he would be safe. The old ravines and the thickets of the swamp would conceal him till night, when he could steal away and leave the country. He could not swim, but he could cross the pond high up by wading. He had not gone three hundred yards, when, as he crossed a rise, he heard his dog's well-known yelp, yelp, and looked back. On the crest of a hill a few hundred yards behind him, he caught sight of the little beast. He was coming on at a gallop, straight on his track, his nose to the ground. A short distance behind him were half-a-dozen men, Hall in the lead. They caught sight of him at the same instant, and a fierce shout went up from them. With a great oath the fugitive rushed on. His heart was thumping against his ribs, and his face burned like fire. He reached a little creek, and, springing in, ran down it through the water. If he could throw the dog from the scent, he might escape. The briars tore his face, and the thorns stuck into his flesh; but he did not feel them. Life was before, death was behind him. He clamored out, and rushed on. A vine caught him and threw him to the ground; a sharp pain shot through his ankle; but he scrambled up, and fled, limping on through the thickets. The water came in sight through the bushes at the foot of the hill he was descending. Perhaps the hound had been thrown from the scent, and he was safe. He wanted but ten minutes. He breathed freer, and paused to listen. Suddenly, however, his hopes were dashed to the ground; for close behind him he heard a noise, and, turning, there was the dog. A fearful oath escaped him. But hope suddenly rose again. He would take him with him. He could drown him in the pond. He turned and called him in a low voice,

"Heah—heah! Come heah, you d—d fool!"

The dog stopped and growled.

He took a few steps back towards him.

"Come heah! Don' you heah me?"

The little beast, with the timidity of his nature intensified, suddenly turned, and, tucking his tail between his legs, retreated some twenty yards, and, half turning around, gave a loud angry bark. A shout answered back in the woods.

With an oath Pokeberry raised and cocked his gun, and brought it up to his shoulder. The little wretch, at the threatening motion, started to flee. There was a loud report. With a yelp the dog rolled over in the bushes, stone-dead.

The living brute fled on again.

In a few moments he was at the water's edge, wading through the alders which grew in the shallows. They were deeper than he had ever seen them. He emerged from the bushes. Only a dozen yards away was the other bank covered with a dense and almost impenetrable thicket. Once there he would be safe. The pursuers were already almost on him. He could hear their voices. Not a moment was to be lost. He could not swim, but the water before him was smooth. He dashed in. and in two steps went down over his head.

He came up choking and struggling, and struck out wildly, only to go down again. Rising again, he beat the water frantically, and again went under; but once more got to the top. His lungs were filled. He was going down again, sinking, drowning. Good God! drowning! He was strangling. Struggling to the top again, he gave a wild cry, "Help, help!"

The water filled his throat, drawing him down, and drowned his despairing shriek.

The men through the bushes only a few yards away heard the cry, wild, agonized, and rushed into the alder thickets, through the water. Parting the bushes, they gazed across to the other bank. It lay calm and quiet in the summer sunshine. They looked at the water just before them. On it, a little way down, just in the current, floated an old worn hat. That was all.

The waters of Newfound slept below as placid as ever.

IT was late the following afternoon. Bruce had been sleeping. He had never recovered complete consciousness; but he was, his uncle said, "doing well." The Major and the Doctor were sitting together on the portico, talking. It seemed as if they could not be separated a moment. The events of a life-time were passing in review; but mainly they dwelt on their boyhood. Mrs. Landon was with them. Margaret had taken her place, and was with Bruce, sitting beside his bed gently fanning him. No one else was in the room. She was dressed in a curious, rich old flowered silk with a high collar and quaint long waist, which she had found in one of the old trunks. It was the counterpart of that in which Mrs. Colonel Landon had had her portrait painted as a bride. Margaret looked in it as if she had stepped out of the old picture over the piano at Landon Hall. She moved from the bedside, and stood looking out of the window. Her profile was clearly defined. It was as fine as a cameo. The setting sun threw its golden rays upon her, and bathed her in its light. Her slender hands were clasped, and her uplifted pensive face wore a sweet gravity. Bruce suddenly opened his eyes. His gaze fell directly on her. He looked at her long and curiously, without stirring.

Presently he said half aloud to himself, "That 's my great-grandmother."

Margaret started, then stepped softly to his side. She noted his improvement, and smiled as she leaned over him.

"Where am I?" asked Bruce.

"At home," she said.

"Am I?"

He glanced around the room; memory seemed trying to reassert itself.

"At home?"

"Yes. Don't talk." Her voice was soft and soothing.

"Can't I talk?" he asked like a child.

"Not just now."

"Why?"

"Well; because I tell you not to: you belong to me." She smiled.

"Do I? Am I my grandfather, then?"

She leaned over and kissed him softly.

"No, my darling, you are your own self, Bruce. But you must not talk now."

"One word. Do you belong to me?" he asked.

"Yes; entirely, with all my heart."

"All right; kiss me; I 'll go to sleep."

A smile of deep content came over his face.

A FEW weeks later there was a small party assembled, one afternoon, on the portico of the old Landon place, Landon Hill. A remarkable transformation had taken place in the time which had elapsed, and as two of the men who were in the party on the porch had ridden up, they had been discussing it in wondering undertones. The old fields which but a few weeks since had been thick with pines were being cleared up; roads were being made; fences built; and whichever way the eye turned, bodies of negroes were at work cutting, clearing, and hauling. Loud laughter and shouts in musical chorus came across the fields from the white-shirted workmen, and volumes of white and blue smoke rose from the piles where the brush was being burned, and, floating away over the fields, gave the landscape the hazy, mellow look of Indian summer.

"Well, this do beat everything," one of the men, the smaller of the two, said to his companion.

The speaker was Jim Hall, just elected sheriff, and the other was Sam Mills, who, owing to the paralysis of Squire Johnson a day or two after the pursuit of Pokeberry, had unexpectedly found himself elected to the honorable position of justice of the peace.

"The Major's a team," said Mills, slowly, as

he took a survey of the scene around them. "He must have half the Landon Hall niggers over here clearin' up."

"He 's a team at gittin' folks elected. If 't had n' been for him, you an' I would n' a beat them lower een fellows so easy," said Hall.

"I 'm glad the Major got the old place back," Mills said slowly, his mind working quietly in the old direction. "He would n' take a heap for it."

"Why, I heard the old Doctor was goin' to stay here, and that Bruce was goin' to stay with him, now he 's married," said Hall, in surprise.

Mills explained:

"So he is. But that 's the same thing. Half the place and half of all the property belongs to the old Doctor and the Major insisted on his takin' it; but he would n't do it and the Major made it over to Bruce an' his wife as a weddin' present. The Major offered him the other place if he wanted it. He 'd give him anything in the world. Bruce havin' it is the same as havin' it himself."

"He certainly ain' stingy," admitted Hall, as they rode into the yard. "The way he looks after the old squa'r shows that, if nothin' else does. You know he went up thar and told him he 'd keep him comfort'ble long as he lived?''

"Yes, so I hearn. Well, I tell you what sort of man the Major is. He 's got a tongue of flame; but he 's got a heart in his body as big as this worl', and he don't bear malice—not a minute.''

They had ridden into the yard and tied their horses.

There, too, they found the work of clearing up performed: the hedges trimmed, the yard cleaned, everything tidy. Bruce, who was lounging on the porch in an easy-chair, beside which sat a young lady, her hand on his arm, came forward to meet them. His companion rose and entered the house. He was still pale, and the bandage was not yet removed from his head. He greeted them cordially, and invited them into the house. The Major met them on the portico. He was followed by the young lady, dressed in a soft white robe, and with an expectant smile in her soft brown eyes, whom he spoke of with evident pride as, "My daughter,'' and to whom he, in turn, presented each of the visitors as, "My friend, Mr. Sam Mills,'' and "My friend, Mr. James Hall.''

Margaret shook hands with them with a manner and a smile which would at once have given her a personal place in their friendship even had she not long held such a position. In a little while there was a step, and the old Doctor came slowly out accompanied by Mrs. Landon. He looked old enough to be the Major's father.

"Brother, these are our two neighbors, Mr. Mills and Mr. Hall, of whom I have spoken to you," said the Major. His voice appeared to the two men to have a new softness in it; a tone of fresh tenderness.

"Oh, I know them," said the old surgeon.

"Yes, we know him," replied the two visitors, and one of them added, "There's many a one down on Newfound knows him too."

Margaret slipped away, and presently returned, followed by two servants, each bearing a large silver waiter, one with tea-things on it, and the other with fruit. One was the old mammy, tall, spare, dignified; the other was Dick Runaway.

"This is an old friend of yours, I believe?" she said, addressing both of the two men, as Dick placed the tray on a little table before her.

Dick's face shone at the reference to him from his mistress, and a double row of very white teeth were suddenly displayed.

After a little the two visitors stated their business. They wanted the Major to run for governor and Bruce for Congress. Newfound would stand by them. Squire Johnson had sent them word he 'd live on purpose to vote for them.

The Major thanked them, but was humorously inexorable in his refusal. He said he had never aspired higher than to be a justice or a constable; he had aspired that high; but there had always been better men found to fill those positions. "The fact is, I am so constituted that if a man disagrees with me I think he has insulted me, and I am not sure that that is the best way for a statesman to feel." Bruce might suit better. Bruce's pretty wife looked proudly at him, and rested a slender white hand on his shoulder.

"All I want," she said, "is that my husband may live here among his own people with the affection of such friends as he has been shown to have these last few weeks and that his friends may know him as I know him."

"Oh! I think we know him on Newfound," said the two delegates, beaming on him. "And we know you too. And if you want anything on Newfound, all you got to do is to call on us and you can get it."

As the two men an hour later rode away

through the evening light, the sky above was a pale, soft blue.

The sun was just disappearing in a haze over the western woods that crowned the horizon beyond the wide bottom, through which, a mile ahead, crept Newfound.

The fields were quiet now; but the rich voices of laughing negroes floated up from the paths by which they wended their way home; the mellowed clangle of cow-bells sounded in the distance, accompanied by the lowing of the cows as they came slowly up to their calves from the pasture by the pond; and a single partridge, on a stump a hundred yards away in the field, piped his three notes of peace to his vagrant mate.

The two men, touched perhaps by the peaceful scene, rode for a little distance without speaking.

Hall first broke the silence.

"Sam," he said, in a low, mysterious tone, "s'pose we run him for governor, anyways. We can git him elected. He 'll git every vote on Newfound."

"I 'm for him for president," said Mills. "Then we 'd have Miss' Landon in the White House, and that would be the best yet—only I don' know what we 'd do without her on New-found."

A homing dove passed close above their heads on the way to its nest; a mocking-bird sang a brief good-night stave of happiness and Newfound settled down beneath the peaceful stars in deep content.

THE END